Beth's leaving ha

But Luke had survived
loneliness.

More than a few times over the years, Beth's face and voice had haunted his dreams. But he'd survived.

Now Beth was back. And Luke didn't know how to feel.

He'd told himself for so long that he hated her. Yet one look into her eyes this afternoon and he'd known hate was the farthest thing from his mind. And that scared him. Terrified him.

The rush of conflicting emotions—love, hate, anger, longing—made him squeeze his eyes shut. Surely those were all old feelings for the girl he used to know. But Beth was a woman now. Thirty-four years old. A mother. A stranger.

Still, Luke wanted, more than anything, for her and their son to be a part of his life.

Dear Reader,

April is the time for the little things...a time for nature to nurture new growth, a time for spring to begin to show its glory.

So, it's perfect timing to have a THAT'S MY BABY! title this month. *What To Do About Baby* by award-winning author Martha Hix is a tender, humorous tale about a heroine who discovers love in the most surprising ways. After her estranged mother's death, the last thing Caroline Grant expected to inherit was an eighteen-month-old sister...or to fall in love with the handsome stranger who delivered the surprise bundle!

And more springtime fun is in store for our readers as Sherryl Woods's wonderful series THE BRIDAL PATH continues with the delightful *Danielle's Daddy Factor*. Next up, Pamela Toth's BUCKLES & BRONCOS series brings you back to the world of the beloved Buchanan brothers when their long-lost sister, Kirby, is found—and is about to discover romance in *Buchanan's Return*.

What is spring without a wedding? *Stop the Wedding!* by Trisha Alexander is sure to win your heart! And don't miss Janis Reams Hudson's captivating story of reunited lovers in *The Mother of His Son*. And a surefire keeper is coming your way in *A Stranger to Love* by Patricia McLinn. This tender story promises to melt your heart!

I hope you enjoy each and every story this month!

Sincerely,

Tara Gavin,
Senior Editor

Please address questions and book requests to:
Silhouette Reader Service
U.S.: 3010 Walden Ave., P.O. Box 1325, Buffalo, NY 14269
Canadian: P.O. Box 609, Fort Erie, Ont. L2A 5X3

JANIS REAMS HUDSON

THE MOTHER OF HIS SON

Silhouette ®

SPECIAL ™ EDITION ®

Published by Silhouette Books
America's Publisher of Contemporary Romance

Special thanks to Carol Pilcher Daly, Ann Benhart,
Frances Greene and Gwen Elam, four special ladies
from Rangely, Colorado, without whom this book
would not have been possible.

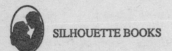 SILHOUETTE BOOKS

ISBN 0-373-24095-3

THE MOTHER OF HIS SON

Copyright © 1997 by Janis Reams Hudson

Books by Janis Reams Hudson

Silhouette Special Edition

Resist Me if You Can #1037
The Mother of His Son #1095

JANIS REAMS HUDSON

Award-winning, bestselling author Janis Reams Hudson spent the first ten years of her life in Rangely, Colorado, where this, her twentieth book, is set. Since then she has lived in California, Texas and Oklahoma, which she now calls home. Her books, both contemporary and historical romances, have appeared on Waldenbooks, B. Dalton and Bookrak bestseller lists, earned numerous awards—including Reviewer's Choice awards from *Romantic Times* and the prestigious National Readers' Choice Award—and been finalists for several other awards, including the RITA Award from Romance Writers of America.

When not writing or researching her next novel, Janis devotes much of her time to various local and national writers' organizations. She currently serves as Immediate Past President and National Literacy Chairperson of Romance Writers of America, the world's largest nonprofit genre writers' organization.

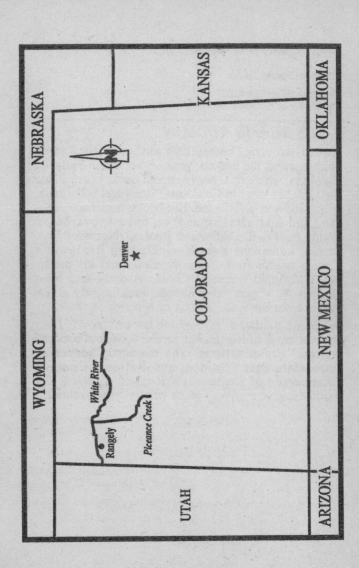

Chapter One

He was giving up.

That was Luke Ryan's personal and professional opinion of his patient's condition. Leon Martin was giving up. Too many bouts of pneumonia these past few years. Too many drinks to drown his sorrows. Too many years alone, with nothing left to do but think about those sorrows.

Damn it all to hell, Luke thought furiously. Leon was only fifty-one years old. Scientifically, biologically, medically speaking, the treatment should be working. It had worked the last time, and the time before that. When this third bout of pneumonia had hit, Leon hadn't been in any worse physical condition than he'd been in last year.

But the man wasn't trying. He was going downhill.

Fast. And Luke could do nothing more than what he was already doing. *Damn you, Leon, fight.*

With a weak movement of his too-thin arm, Leon motioned Luke closer. His lips moved.

Luke leaned down. "What is it, Leon? What did you say?"

The man moistened his dry, cracked lips with the tip of his tongue. "Beth. I want…to see Beth."

The sudden pain in Luke's gut made him feel like he'd been kicked by a mule. It was like that every time someone mentioned her name, which most folks took care not to do around him.

"I want…my baby, Luke. Wanna…see her."

Luke swallowed the bitter taste in his mouth. "I hear you, Leon. I just don't know how to help. I don't know where she is, you know that."

A fierce light flashed in Leon's eyes. The first real sign of life Luke had seen in days. "The Old Witch knows," Leon said in a surprisingly strong voice for a man who could barely speak a moment ago.

Luke met his gaze. "Rose? Rose knows where Beth is?"

"Always…has." The brief spurt of energy was gone. "Make her tell you, Luke. I want…to see my baby."

Luke placed a hand on Leon's arm and straightened. "I'll talk to Rose."

"Promise?"

"I promise."

As Luke walked down the hill from the hospital after dark that night, he acknowledged the churning in his gut for what it was. Rage. Pure unadulterated rage. And it surprised him. He thought he'd dealt with it years ago.

But seeing a big, strong man like Leon Martin give up on life made him furious. At Leon. At the inadequacies of medical science. At life. If Leon didn't start fighting, he was going to die, and there wasn't a damn thing Luke could do about it. Unless he could somehow locate Beth Martin. If she condescended to grace the town of Rangely with her presence, maybe she could boost her father's spirits enough to make him want to live.

The cloud of rage grew thicker around him. If Rose Shoemaker knew where her granddaughter was, Luke would find a way to make her tell. The traitorous little bitch would come and sit by her father's bedside if Luke had to drag her back to town and tie her to the damn hospital bed.

He stopped at the foot of Rose's driveway and took a deep breath of cool night air. Her house was one street over from his. The two streets, South and Magnolia, were connected by a short cross street called, appropriately enough, Short Street. But Short connected more than South and Magnolia. It connected Luke's driveway to Rose's, where he now stood.

It had always galled him to look out the front of his house and see hers. He'd damn near decided against buying the place just because of that. Yet he'd liked the house. In the end he had decided to hell with her. Maybe looking out her front door and seeing his house would irritate her, and if so, that was fine with him.

Now, for the first time in all the years they'd been neighbors, he was walking to her door. If not for

Leon, Luke would quite frankly just as soon have run naked down Main Street in a blizzard. He did *not* like this woman.

He had to get himself under control. From his earliest memories, Rose Shoemaker had always treated him like something to be wiped off the bottom of her shoe. Luke had tried not to take it personally, but she seemed to have a special dislike—okay, call it what it was, hatred—for him. All because he'd had the nerve, at the tender age of six, to fall in love with her granddaughter.

He knew if he closed his eyes, he could still picture Bethany Martin as she'd looked back then in first grade, all eyes and freckles and skinned knees, her long, dark hair forced into tortured ringlets that bounced when she walked and fell straight by the end of the day.

It had been love at first sight. For both of them.

Luke shook his head at the foolish memories, but they wouldn't go away. He saw her as if in a family photo album, year by year, growing, maturing, turning more beautiful every day. In his innocence, he hadn't realized what it all meant. Until high school, when she'd turned all sleek and shapely and sexy enough to make a young man's blood rush. And she had been his. All his.

Until that day sixteen years ago, when she and her mother went off on vacation and never came back.

She's got more important things to do with her life than waste herself on a no-account like you and this pitiful excuse of a town.

Rose Shoemaker had practically glowed with triumph when she'd made that announcement to Luke on the sidewalk in front of the First Baptist Church one Sunday morning.

Luke shook away the memories. All that was a long time ago. Beth was gone. Good riddance. Her leaving had nearly killed him, but he had survived. He had a good life and was content.

And now he had to bring her back.

But a moment later, standing in Rose Shoemaker's doorway because she wouldn't let him across the threshold—which didn't surprise him one damn bit— Luke wasn't sure just how he was going to accomplish the goal of getting Beth Martin to her father's bedside.

"Absolutely not." The bitter old woman clamped her lips shut so hard and fast on the words that her jowls quivered.

If she had a dog, Luke thought distractedly, and if people really looked like their dogs, Rose would have a bulldog. A mean, ugly one, with beady little eyes and a burr up its...

No, that wasn't right. Not in looks. But personality, definitely.

"This is just another one of Leon's tricks, the worthless bum."

"It's no trick, Rose. He's not responding to the medication. He's giving up."

The old woman simply stared at him, her lips pressed together, one eyebrow arched in disdain.

"He's dying, Rose."

A flicker of doubt crossed her faded eyes. "He is not."

In the end, Luke had to drag her to the hospital,

straight into Leon's room, before she would believe the seriousness of the situation.

"Good God," she whispered.

If he weren't so damned worried about Leon, Luke would have been impressed that anything on earth could faze Rose Shoemaker as Leon's gray, emaciated appearance obviously did.

"All right," she said, her voice shaking. "You've convinced me. I'll call." Then she steadied herself and shot Luke a cold gaze. "But she won't come."

Beth and Ryan were loading the last of the dinner dishes into the dishwasher when the phone rang.

"I'll get it." Ryan was closest to the phone. "Maybe it's Gran, calling to tell us when she'll be home."

Beth gave her son a droll look. He didn't for a minute think it was his grandmother on the phone, nor did he wish it was. It was probably one of his friends.

A moment later she knew better.

"Oh, hi, Grandma Rose. Gee, Gran's not here. She left for Branson this morning with the ladies from next door. Sure, here." He held the phone toward Beth. "Grandma Rose wants to talk to you. I'm gonna go catch some MTV."

Beth took the phone from her son's hand, curious as to why her grandmother would call during the week. "Hi, Grandma."

"Bethany, dear, when do you expect your mother home?"

"Not till next week. She just left this morning."

"Oh, my. I'm afraid we don't have that much time. Is there a number where I can reach her?"

"No," Beth answered. "She and her friends were playing it loose. She said she'd call in a day or two and let us know where she was. What's wrong, Grandma?"

"Well, honey, I know you won't want to hear this, but...it's your father."

The tiny pain in the region of Beth's heart was sharp. "Daddy? What's happened?"

As her grandmother spoke, Beth began to tremble. Her father? Not expected to live?

No matter how many times during the past sixteen years Beth had told herself she had no feelings left for a father who had turned his back on her, she had known deep inside she was lying to herself. The news of his condition, and that he was asking for her, told her so. The woman she had become might want to ignore his plea, but the little girl in her could not.

Daddy, Daddy, why didn't you want me anymore?

The ancient question, though it burned deeply in her heart, was suddenly irrelevant. He wanted her now. And if she didn't go to him, she might never have the chance to ask him why he had stopped loving her.

"What..." Beth paused to clear her throat. "What about Mother?"

Her grandmother's voice came back stiff. "He didn't ask for her. Since she's not home anyway, I suppose you'll just have to wait until she returns and tell her yourself. I'm sure she won't want you to come, dear, and I certainly can't blame you for wanting to stay away. I just felt obligated, under the circumstances, to tell you what was happening.''

"Grandma, of course I'm coming. He's my father.''

"We'll wait and see what your mother says, dear.''

Beth gripped the phone more tightly. "I'm thirty-four years old, Grandma. I stopped asking Mother's permission a long time ago. I'll see you soon.''

"You can't just take off like that, Bethany. What about your job? Ryan? You have responsibilities.''

"If you didn't want me to come, why did you call?''

"Well, I...I just thought you should know, that's all. I certainly didn't think you'd want to come back here after all this time. After the way he treated you, why would you want to see him now?''

Beth had always thought of her mother's mother as a cold woman, but to suggest Beth not go see her father when he was dying, to suggest that Beth would want to turn her back on the man who had carried her on his shoulders and let her hang on to his ears as they galloped around the yard, the man who had taught her to fish, the man who, for all her childhood years, had kept the boogeyman away—no, Beth could not stay away.

"Maybe,'' she told her grandmother softly, "it's time I asked him what went wrong. I'll see you soon, Grandma.''

With her grandmother's harsh voice still grating over the line, Beth gently hung up the phone. Her own words to her grandmother rang in her ears. Yes, it was time to ask the question. Past time.

Over the years Beth had told herself that the trouble

had been solely between her parents. She knew her mother had been increasingly unhappy during the two years before she and Beth had left Rangely. Whatever had gone wrong, Beth had assured herself it had nothing to do with her, except by default. She bore a strong physical resemblance to her mother. Maybe her father simply had not wanted a living reminder of the woman he no longer loved.

But deep inside, Beth harbored the fear that it *had* been her fault, whatever "it" was. Her father had stopped loving her, didn't want her any longer.

Luke, too, had no longer wanted her.

Luke.

After all this time, his name still had the power to rip her peace, her heart, to shreds.

From the living room came the sound of Ryan's laughter over something on the television.

Beth's stomach tightened. Ryan. Dear heaven, what was she to do about Ryan? But there was really no question. It was time for Ryan to meet his grandfather, before it was too late.

"Ryan?" Beth stepped into the living room. "Something's come up. I need to talk to you."

Too keyed up over the conversation with her grandmother to sleep, Beth decided not to bother trying. With each passing moment her nerves stretched more taut. Closing her eyes would be an exercise in futility.

Picking up on his mother's nerves, Ryan was nearly as wired as Beth. He finished packing in short order, then hauled out the *Rand McNally Road Atlas* and plotted their course. A route Beth had taken only once in her life, sixteen years ago. That time, she'd been traveling west to east, never dreaming she'd be gone from Rangely more than a couple of weeks. Now, all these years later, she was going back.

Barely more than an hour after receiving her grandmother's call, Beth and Ryan left the lights of Kansas City behind and headed west into the night on I-70. Their trip would be a straight shot all the way across Kansas and Colorado to Rifle on the Western Slope, less than a hundred miles shy of the Utah border. From Rifle it would be another forty miles to Meeker, then fifty-five more to Rangely. A total of nearly nine hundred miles that, if they drove straight through, would take them fourteen or fifteen hours. That would put them in Rangely around noon or one tomorrow.

She was foolish to have started out so late at night, much less to even consider driving all night, then all morning. But if they had waited until morning to leave, they would have reached Rangely late at night. Even worse, if they stopped for the night, it would be another whole day before they made it. If her father's condition was bad enough to warrant her grandmother even mentioning his name in passing, much less making a special call in the middle of the week when rates were higher, then Beth wasn't willing to wait.

Rose Shoemaker usually wouldn't even answer a question about Leon Martin, wouldn't so much as allow his name to soil her lips, let alone talk to the man.

That's why her call tonight had been so startling. Knowing how her grandmother felt about her father, Beth wouldn't have been surprised to have heard nothing from her until it was too late. Grandma had always been adamant that Leon Martin was a low-class loser not worthy of the time of day.

So why should Grandma suddenly care that he was asking for his daughter?

The spaghetti Beth had fixed for dinner burned in her stomach. After having no contact with her father for sixteen years—at his request—she knew a sudden, overwhelming need to get to him as fast as possible. She could not arrive too late. She simply could not.

"Mom? What do you think Gran will do when she gets your message?"

A good question. What would her mother do? "I don't know, honey."

"Do you think he'll like me?"

Beth heard the uncertainty in her son's attempted casualness. She heard something else, too, something like longing, and she ached for the boy who'd grown up with no men in his life. No father, no grandfather, no brothers or uncles. Not even any *uncles,* she thought wryly.

"What's not to like?" she asked. "Your grandfather will love you."

The June night sped past the windows, with flashes of lights from other cars and scattered farms. Traffic was thin out in the country on a weeknight, with the usual exception of eighteen-wheelers freighting goods to and from Kansas City.

Ryan fiddled with the radio until he found his favorite Kansas City hard rock station, then settled back against the seat. He flopped one foot across the opposite knee and drummed his fingers against his shoe in time with the music.

After a few minutes he fell still. "Mom?"

"Mmmm?"

"Will we...that is, uh...do you think...my dad will be around? That we might...uh, run into him? I mean, maybe he's moved back there by now."

Beth felt her heart climb right up into her throat. Sweat made her hands slip on the steering wheel. "I doubt he'll be there, honey. The last time Grandma Rose even mentioned his name was years ago when he left town."

From the corner of her eye she saw him gnaw his lower lip and pick at a hangnail.

Had she done the right thing all these years in not bringing Ryan and his father together? The question, as always, ate at her.

As if Ryan had read her mind, he said, "I think I'd rather not have him know about me at all, instead of finding out for sure he didn't want anything to do with me."

"Oh, honey."

"Except," he said grimly, "I'd sure like to see the look on his face when I punch his lights out for what he did to you."

Beth's hands clenched around the steering wheel.

Chapter Two

Beth wasn't expecting much as she neared Rangely the next day. Sixteen years would have brought a lot of changes, and none of them for the better, she was sure. She knew the old saying, "You can't go home again." But that was all right. She wasn't trying to go home. She was just going to see her father. Home was Kansas City, Missouri, not Rangely, Colorado.

Her memories of Rangely, she knew, were tinted by all those wonderful years before her life had taken such a drastic turn. The mile-long Main Street that she had known like the back of her hand wouldn't be nearly as wide as she remembered. The stores and shops and offices had probably all turned seedy with time and neglect. She was prepared for whatever she found. It wouldn't mean anything to her. Not after all these years.

But she wasn't prepared for the lake. "Where did that come from?" she heard herself ask.

"Is it new?" Ryan asked.

"I...well, it wasn't here when I lived here." The sign read Kenney Reservoir. Taylor Draw Dam. "There used to be ranches here." She searched her memory, trying to remember the families who'd lived along this section of the White River. The Powells— good grief, their ranch was gone. She wondered what had become of them, if any of them still lived in the area, how they and the other families felt about losing their homes to progress.

Still, she could imagine the importance of a reliable water source for the area. More than once during her childhood the river had frozen solid and the town's water had been cut off to a brown, muddy trickle.

The recreational aspects of the lake should help the area, too. The kids and boaters and fishermen in the county must be in hog heaven. Not that Beth remembered ever feeling a lack of things to do in Rangely. But a lake! The possibilities were endless!

She was almost to town when the new airport on her right kept her from glancing left toward the road up Douglas Creek. The road to Ryan Ranch. Luke's ranch.

No point thinking about it.

Then she was beyond the Douglas turnoff, beyond the airport and the new brick water plant, and coming up on that last hill before town. As she passed the Episcopal church on the left and crested the hill, she caught sight of the clean, broad swath of Main, all one mile of it, cutting through what, from this angle, looked like a solid, stunning, *green* grove of trees.

Her breath caught. All that green? In the middle of nothing other than sagebrush, greasewood and piñon scattered across otherwise bare, rocky ground bleached white by sun and wind and time? The place couldn't have changed that much.

Then she was down the hill, and all those deceptive treetops were back in perspective.

Ah, darn. It looked as if Eddy's Café was long gone. But look! Nichols! And across the street, Bestway. She wondered if, in this day and age, people could still sign for their groceries at Bestway.

"I guess we're getting close to town, huh?" Ryan asked, studying the buildings up and down the street that was, surprisingly, even wider and cleaner and neater than Beth remembered.

She chuckled at his comment. "Not close," she told him. "This is Main Street. We're right smack-dab in the middle of town."

Her son gave her a crooked grin. "I was afraid you were gonna say that."

The stoplight at the intersection ahead where Beth intended to turn left appalled her. A stoplight? On Main Street? How were the kids supposed to drag Main if they had to sit and wait on a stoplight? But then, she figured that was probably the main reason for the light.

When the signal turned green, Beth headed south on White and drove straight for the hospital. As they passed Magnolia Street she pointed out Grandma Rose's house.

Just up the hill she turned right toward the hospital attached to the back of the clinic and pulled in beneath the shade provided by a row of tall elms. The short-lived jubilation from seeing her hometown again faded fast. Exhaustion from driving all night caught up to her with a vengeance. Exhaustion, and something else that felt suspiciously like fear.

Yes, fear was exactly what she felt.

She had come to see the man who, for the first eighteen years of her life, had been the center of her world.

Well, okay, so he'd been the center for only about the first six—until she'd met and fallen in love with Luke Ryan right there in the second row from the door in Mrs. Drake's first-grade class. Luke Ryan. Friend, sweetheart, lover. Heartbreaker.

Regardless of what she had felt for Luke, Leon Martin had still been her hero, was still her father. Now he was sick, maybe dying. And he had asked to see her.

And she had questions.

She shut her eyes and took a deep breath for courage. Then, before she could change her mind and turn the car around and head back out of town, she threw open the door and got out. On the sidewalk she paused to give her stomach a chance to unclench.

Ryan met her there. "Nervous?"

"Yes," she admitted. "You?"

He stuffed his hands into his jeans pockets and hunched his shoulders. "Yeah. I guess."

After another deep breath, Beth put her arm around his shoulders and started toward the door. "Come on. Let's go meet your grandfather."

The lobby of the hospital was quiet, tasteful and empty. The receptionist behind a glass window across from the door told her where to find her father. "Take the hall to the left. Mr. Martin is in the first room on the left.''

With hands and knees shaking, the best Beth could give the woman was a slight nod of thanks.

The leather soles of her flats made a slight slapping sound on the tile floor. Ryan's running shoes squeaked.

The room the receptionist had directed them to was across from the nurses' station, which was currently unmanned. Or was it unnursed? Beth wondered with a nervous chuckle. Holding Ryan's hand tightly in hers for courage, she stepped into her father's room.

Her first thought was that the receptionist had made a mistake. This was the wrong room. That thin, hollow-cheeked, sunken-eyed, gray-skinned man hooked up to more than a few tubes and machines could not possibly be her big, strapping father. She took a step back and stumbled against Ryan.

"Mom?"

The man on the bed—the *old* man, *ancient* man—opened his eyes.

Beth's hand flew to her mouth to cover her gasping cry.

The man squinted against the light that shone in his eyes from above the bed. "Margaret?" His voice sounded like rusty pipes.

Beth blinked and tried to swallow, but the lump in her throat was too big. "It's me, Daddy. Beth."

His lips trembled; his face twisted with anguish. "Beth? You came? You really came?"

The stunned joy in his voice and eyes took her breath away. She'd come to ask questions, to demand answers. What questions? What answers? In that moment none of it mattered compared to the sudden terror that overwhelmed her. Dear God, if she'd waited so much as another day or two, she might very well have been too late.

"Oh, Daddy!" Beth dropped Ryan's hand and ran to the bed. Her father reached for her, and she fell against his chest, soaking it instantly with the tears she couldn't hold back. An arm encircled her back and hugged her with surprising strength. "Oh, Daddy, Daddy!"

While he was definitely thin and gaunt, she was gratified to realize his body didn't seem as frail as she'd thought. She used that knowledge to steady herself, and after a few moments was able to straighten and wipe her tears.

Her father was staring past her shoulder as if in shock. "What is it?" she asked tensely. Beth followed his gaze. The only thing in sight was Ryan, standing just inside the door, shuffling from one foot to the other, his eyes suspiciously red rimmed, lashes damp.

"My God," her father whispered. "He's... He's... Is he...yours?"

Beth's smile was wobbly as she held out her hand toward her son. "Well, sometimes I claim him. This is Ryan, Daddy. Ryan, come meet your grandfather."

As Ryan came hesitantly closer, her father's eyes grew bigger, rounder. "Your...son?" he said in wonder.

The closer Beth looked at her father, the more suspicion bloomed. It couldn't be, but he looked as though... She sucked in a sharp breath. "You didn't know I had a son?"

His gaze still glued to his grandson, Leon shook his head slowly from side to side. "I had no...idea."

Shocked, but unable to deny the equally shocked look on her father's face, Beth stumbled for something to say. "Surely Grandma would have told you," she cried.

Leon squeezed his eyes shut. Tears spilled down his cheeks. "Not a word. Not one damn word did she tell me." The sudden strength in his voice took her by surprise. "Come here, boy. Let me get a better look at you."

The closer Ryan got, the wider Leon grinned. "Well, girl, we know where you got him, don't we? He's the spittin' image of his daddy, all right. Ryan, did you say? Well, don't that beat all."

The sudden cheery chuckle in his voice, coming so close on the heels of all the other raw emotions in the room, left Beth reeling.

"How old are you?"

"Fifteen, sir."

"Is that too old to hug your granddad?"

With an awkward shrug, Ryan smiled. "I don't know. I never had a granddad before."

"Well, then." Leon cleared his throat and steadied his voice. "What do ya say we give it a try, huh?"

The sight of her nearly grown son hugging his grandfather for the first time sent tears streaming down Beth's cheeks again. Her throat closed, her chest tightened.

She could tell the emotional trauma was wearing her father out. After a few minutes of small talk, she sent Ryan out to find a pop machine. "If we tire you out too much, they might not let us come back," she told her father with a teary smile.

"You're not leaving, are you?" he protested.

"You're not well, Daddy. I'll stay until you go to sleep, if you want. Then we'll come back tomorrow."

"No, tonight."

Beth smiled. "All right, tonight, then."

"You promise?"

She took his hand in hers and squeezed. "I promise."

"You look a little tired yourself," he told her, "but you're sure a sight for these old eyes."

"So are you," she said with a tight swallow.

"You promise you'll come back?" he asked anxiously.

"Wild horses couldn't keep me away."

Slugging down a cold pop, Ryan braced one foot and his back against the corner where the hall from the reception area met the hall leading to the patients' rooms. The nurse now behind the counter at the nursing station gave him a curious smile.

Wow, Ryan thought. He'd met his grandfather.

Ryan was mortified that he hadn't been able to keep from crying, but then, everybody else had been bawling, too, so he figured maybe his own tears hadn't been that big a deal after all.

He took another swig, then a deep breath, and realized he felt pretty darned good about meeting his grandfather. He just wished, for his mother's sake, that Granddad wasn't so sick.

From down the hall, past where he and his mother had come in, he heard a low rumble of voices, then laughter. A doctor in a white lab coat and a guy in jeans and cowboy boots, who looked a couple of years older than Ryan and had one bandaged arm in a sling, came out of a room and into the hall. Something about the pair snared Ryan's attention.

"Thanks for not calling Dad," the teenager told the doctor.

"Don't thank me," the doctor answered as the two walked slowly in Ryan's direction. "It would have been easier on you if I'd called. Now you're going to have to explain how you ended up with half a dozen stitches in your arm."

The boy grimaced. "Maybe I'll just tell Kat and let her tell Dad."

The doctor laughed. "Smart move, kid. You must take after your uncle."

The boy grinned. "That's what Dad says every time I do something ornery."

But the doctor was no longer listening. He was staring at Ryan, his head cocked to one side. He stood less than five feet away from where Ryan still leaned against the corner.

Uneasy under the man's frowning gaze, Ryan straightened. Maybe there was some rule against leaning on the walls around this place.

"Don't I know you?" the doctor asked Ryan.

"No, sir. I'm just here visiting."

From the reception area a guy's voice called out, "Hey, Ryan."

The doctor, the boy with the bandaged arm and Ryan Martin all turned at once. Their three voices sounded in unison, "Yeah?"

Stunned, the three looked at each other. Then Ryan

noticed the doctor's name tag. His gaze shot up to the man's face, and he couldn't seem to stop staring. He felt all hot and trembly inside and couldn't catch his breath.

The smiling nurse behind the counter chuckled. "What a small world. His name ought to be Ryan. He looks enough like Mike to be his brother."

Ryan jerked his gaze to the boy with the bandaged arm, suddenly realizing what had first caught his attention. It was scary as hell. It was like looking in the mirror at his own face.

He tore his gaze from the boy and looked at the doctor again. The name tag. The face. Oh. Oh, God.

Ryan sidled toward the door of his grandfather's room. "Mom?" His mouth went dry. His heart knocked around inside his chest as if it might bust loose any minute. With an outstretched arm he finally felt the open doorway he sought. "Mom?" Breathless, he slid around the doorway, the doctor following him step for step, pale, shocked, staring at him out of eyes so like Ryan's own, it was eerie. "Mom, is it him?"

At Ryan's question, Beth stiffened and forced herself to turn toward the door. Shock held her immobile. Her lungs froze.

"It's him, isn't it." Ryan didn't phrase it as a question. The look on his mother's face, the way she turned pale as milk, the way her hand shook as it rose to her chest told him he was right.

The doctor looked just as shocked.

And he was. Luke Ryan felt as if he'd been chopped off at the knees. With a dull ax. The muscles in his chest constricted, leaving him struggling to draw in air.

Beth.

He thought he'd prepared himself for his first sight of her in sixteen years. He thought he'd be able to remember the way she'd walked out on him, leaving his heart bleeding, shredded into a million irreparable pieces.

He did remember. The pain was there, clear and sharp as though he were hearing again for the first time that she was never coming home.

But he hadn't counted on her looking as if she hadn't aged a day. He'd entertained fantasies over the years, when he'd allowed himself to think of her at all, that she had run to fat, or turned to skin and bones, old and haggard and ugly before her time. That maybe she'd grown a wart on the end of her nose.

Never once had he thought those soft, gray-green eyes would still have the power to pull him into their depths, or that her generous lips above that dainty, pointed chin, lips now parted in shock, could still make his knees shake after all these years.

He clenched his hands at his sides. Her effect on him didn't matter. Couldn't. She'd carved him up into little pieces and left him for dead.

Now, sixteen years later, she'd walked back into his life. And she hadn't come alone. He tore his gaze from her beautiful, treacherous face to stare in awe, in shock, at the boy before him. "My God" was all he could manage.

With pure venom in his face, in his voice, the boy sneered at Luke. "Hi, *Daddy.*"

Ryan watched, heart thundering, as the man before

him finally realized who he was looking at. Ryan was shaking so hard he was surprised he didn't just fall down. He'd told himself all his life that if he ever got the chance to meet this man, he'd get even. Could he do it? Here was his chance, but did he have the guts to take it?

Something Gran had said last week came to mind. Her announcement about going to Branson with friends had come out of the blue. As far back as Ryan could remember, Gran never went anywhere or did anything that didn't involve him and his mom. Mom had said something to her, and Gran had answered, "Most of the things in life that we regret are not things we do, but things we don't do."

Standing in his grandfather's hospital room, with his mother in shock and this man standing before him, Ryan thought about it and realized Gran was right. If he didn't take his shot now, he'd regret it for the rest of his life.

He took a deep breath, braced his feet and plowed his right fist into Dr. Luke Ryan's mouth.

"That," Ryan said with narrowed eyes as he massaged his aching hand, "is for what you did to my mother."

Chapter Three

Sharp pain and the copper taste of blood exploded in Luke's mouth. He reeled under the impact of the blow.

Horrified, Beth shrieked her son's name.

Mike stood at the door and gaped. "Uncle Luke?"

The nurse rushed from her station to the doorway. "Doctor?"

And from the bed came an unmistakable hoot of half horror, half laughter, followed instantly by a fit of strangled coughing and choking.

Oh, God, oh, God. A woman he had loved more than anything, whom he hadn't set eyes on in sixteen years. A son he'd never even dreamed existed. And a patient who needed his immediate attention.

Leon's coughing snapped Luke out of whatever craziness had let him walk through the door of this room in the first place. He should have known what he'd find. One look at the boy's face and he should have known. Had known, really, just hadn't been able to believe it.

But he'd talked to Rose only last night. Until he'd walked into this room he hadn't really been certain the old bat would call Beth at all, but she must have, because less than sixteen hours later, Bethany Martin, or whatever her name was these days, had arrived.

And she hadn't come alone.

Her son. Good God. *Their* son. His and Beth's.

The coughing from the bed grew worse.

Luke jerked into action and rushed to Leon's side. "Connie, clear this room."

In less than two seconds Beth found herself and Ryan out in the hall, the door to her father's room shut firmly in her face, that frightful hacking and strangling echoing down the hall. The boy with the bandaged arm was staring at Ryan as if seeing a ghost.

For courage, and to reassure herself her son was all right, she took Ryan's hand.

He winced and drew back.

Carefully she lifted his hand and studied the reddened knuckles. "Did you hurt yourself?"

With his eyes filled with uncertainty, Ryan nevertheless stuck out his chin. "I'm not sorry I hit him."

That lump was back in her throat. She smoothed a hand over his cheek. "I know, sweetheart. I'm not angry. I guess you had a right."

"It wasn't for me." He shook his head. "It was for you. For what he did to you."

"Who *are* you people? Why'd you hit my uncle?"

Beth turned, standing beside her son who was half a head taller than she was, and faced the boy. "Luke is your uncle?" She searched his face, easily seeing the resemblance. All the Ryan men strongly favored each other. Same dark brown hair, same square, stubborn jaw, same full, firm mouth. "Are you...oh, my. You can't be Mike. Not J.D.'s Mike."

The boy frowned. "I'm Mike Ryan, and J.D.'s my dad. Who're you?"

Despite the circumstances of the past few traumatic moments, Beth couldn't help the smile that came to her. "I'm Beth Martin, and this is my son, Ryan. But you can't be Mike Ryan." At his puzzled look, her smile grew. "The last time I saw Mike Ryan he was two years old and had chocolate smeared from ear to ear."

He stepped closer, peering at her intently. Then his eyes widened. "You're the one in the picture."

"The picture?"

He gave a loose shrug. "You know, one of those pictures your parents pull out for company just to embarrass you. It was my second birthday and, just like you said, I had chocolate all over me. There was Mom and Dad and me. Mom was holding Sandy, 'cause she was just a baby. Uncle Luke and you were there, too."

Beth closed her eyes on a sharp intake of breath and felt her stomach tremble. "I remember," she whispered. She opened her eyes. Her smile this time wobbled slightly. "You must be, what, eighteen now?"

"Yes, ma'am." He looked at Ryan. "Are you... Why did you call Luke 'Dad'?"

Beth felt the tension vibrate through Ryan.

She hadn't realized the coughing and choking coming from her father's room had quieted, nor had she heard the door behind her open. But she heard Luke's deep voice from directly behind her when he said, "Looks to me, that's what I am. I believe that makes the two of you cousins."

Beth forced herself to loosen the nearly crippling grip she had on Ryan's hand. She couldn't believe how calm Luke sounded. The very ease with which he spoke, the casual, careless way he acknowledged Ryan as his son, made her want to gouge his eyes out. But rather than confront him there in the hall, before her son, Mike and an all-too-observant nurse, she tugged Ryan's hand and tried to step past Luke toward her father's room.

"No." Luke caught her by the arm. "I gave him a sedative. He went out like a light. You can see him again this evening. If you plan to stick around that long."

Biting back a scream of pure rage—how *dare* he touch her!—Beth slowly turned her head to face him. "Let go of—"

The look in his eyes cut off her words, her breath. He might have sounded indifferent, but she'd never seen such cold wrath in her life as she saw in his eyes.

"I think you and I need to talk."

His eerily calm voice with those seething eyes made her want to cringe. Instead, she tossed her head. "We have nothing to say to each other."

"Oh, I think maybe we do." With his hand clamped around her arm, he started down the hall.

"Connie, I imagine this young man could use something cold on his knuckles. Mike," he called over his shoulder, "entertain your cousin. We'll be in my office."

Beth thought about resisting, about yanking her arm free of his grasp, grabbing Ryan and running. She thought about it, and discarded the idea. This confrontation was sixteen years overdue. Maybe once she'd had the chance to tell him *exactly* what she thought of him, some of the guilt she carried for never telling him about his son would lift. And maybe the pain, too. The pain of not understanding how Luke could have done what he did to her. The guilt of feeling as though she had in some way cheated her son out of a father.

Luke took her up the hall past a large examination room and into the clinic portion of the facilities. He pushed open the door beneath a small sign that read Luke Ryan, M.D.

Luke, a doctor. The idea was startling. All these years she had pictured him out on the ranch raising sheep or cattle. Raising children. With her best friend.

His office was small. Most of the floor space was taken up by a desk covered with file folders. Two visitors' chairs were wedged between the front of the desk and the wall it faced. The wall next to the door and the one behind the desk were covered with floor-to-cciling bookcases. The wall beside his desk bore diplomas and certificates in skinny black frames. Behind the two guest chairs hung a framed, enlarged photograph of hills and bluffs dotted in sage, greasewood and juniper. Beth ached with memories of traipsing those very hills with Luke and his brother, J.D., a lifetime ago.

Luke closed the office door behind them and stood before it, as though on guard to keep her from running out. Moments ago his face had been pale. Now it was dark as sin, flushed with anger. His eyes, so like her son's, practically shot fire at her.

"Why, Beth?"

The harshness of his demand flayed her already taut nerves.

"Good God, he's my *son!* How could you keep him from me all these years? How could you not even tell me about him?"

Beth braced herself against the anguish and fury in his voice. She had her own anguish, her own fury. "Tell you about him?" She flexed her fingers at her sides, reliving the dark horror of those days sixteen years ago. Bitterness swamped her and came out in the form of a sharp laugh. "What was I supposed to do, interrupt your wedding to let you know you'd managed to get both of us knocked up?"

"What wedding?"

"You've had so many you can't remember that first one?"

"Why the hell would you say something like that? I've never been married."

"Never been... What kind of fool do you take me for? I heard all about the announcement and the pictures in the paper. Did you think because I was out of town I wouldn't know? What were you planning to do if I'd come home from that vacation with my mother? How were you going to explain what you'd done?"

Luke listened with growing amazement and bewilderment. His first thought was that she was throwing out a smoke screen to keep from having to explain why she'd never told him about his son. But the look in her eyes, so full of pain, of betrayal, told him otherwise.

He understood the betrayal. He felt it, too. It sliced into him with razor sharpness, deep, killing deep. He'd been feeling the bite for sixteen years.

But an announcement? Pictures in the paper? "Beth, I don't have any idea what you're talking about."

"All right," she cried, her voice, her whole body shaking so hard Luke feared she might collapse. "You want me to say it out loud, I'll say it. I'm talking about you marrying my best friend before I even had a chance to come home from vacation."

Dumbfounded with shock, Luke stared at her. "Carol? You think I—"

"I don't *think* anything. I *know*."

"Obviously you don't. Are you saying you never told me about my son because you thought I married Carol? That *that's* why you never came back?"

"Married her because you got her pregnant, just like you did me."

"If you had bothered to come home any time in the last *sixteen years*, you'd know better. Hell, if you'd so much as picked up the phone and called—"

"Damn you," Beth cried. "Don't lie to me. Not now, not after all this time."

Luke reeled. She believed it! Good God, she actually believed the crazy things she was saying. "Beth, I never married Carol. I never married anyone.

Carol has been married to Jerry Howard since the summer after we graduated from high school. They have a fifteen-year-old daughter.''

Beth staggered backward into the corner where the bookcases met. "No," she whispered. "No." If he was telling the truth, dear God...

"Are you telling me," Luke demanded, "that you didn't come home that summer because you honestly believed I could have married your best friend? That I could have married *anyone* but you? You kept my son from me all these years, you let..." He stopped to swallow, his eyes screaming a pain so deep it made her tremble. "You let some other man raise my son? Were you *out of your mind?*"

Beth's ears rang. The room tilted. Darkness crept along the outer edges of her vision. "You've...never been married?"

"Never."

Even if he hadn't spoken with such firmness, hadn't spoken at all, Beth would have had her answer. The truth was unmistakable in his eyes.

She felt her head hit the shelf behind her, felt her knees start to give. She heard a harsh oath, then hands, big, strong hands, had her by the waist.

Movement. The backs of her knees against something cool and firm. Then relief as Luke lowered her onto the leather chair behind his desk, followed by astonishment when he pulled her head down toward her knees.

Another oath, followed by her name.

"I'm all right." She tried to push the hands, those warm, wonderful hands, away. "I'm all right."

"The hell you are. Be still."

She tried to inhale. "This is a myth, you know," she told him, surprised by the strength and humor in her voice.

One of those hands, gentle now, rubbed her back. "Don't talk just yet."

"I mean it. I'm not going to pass out unless you make me stay like this."

"Hush, I'm a doctor, remember?"

"Yeah, and you guys are all alike. I can't breathe all scrunched up like this, Doctor."

"Okay, but take it slow." With a hand to her shoulder, he helped her sit up.

Beth slumped against the back of the chair, closed her eyes and took a deep breath.

"Better?"

She licked her lips and nodded, not yet daring to look at him. Not yet ready to face the truth in his eyes.

"You look tired. You must have gotten up at the crack of dawn and caught the first flight to Grand Junction to get here so quick. I only spoke with your grandmother about calling you last night."

She did open her eyes then, to find him on one knee next to her. She gave him a wry smile. "Guess again, Doctor. We drove. By dawn we'd been on the road about eight hours."

She saw a dozen questions shoot across his eyes, but she wasn't prepared for the one that came out. "What happened sixteen years ago, Beth? Why didn't you come home?"

She closed her eyes and swallowed. She'd never thought of having to explain. What could she tell him that would make sense, that would justify in his mind her desertion and fifteen lost years of his son's life? She stared at him dully. "It's a long story."

He rose, then rounded the desk and sat on one of the chairs there. "I'm not going anywhere." The look in his eyes hardened. "And neither are you, until I get some answers."

Answers? she thought hysterically. She was supposed to have answers? All she had were questions. More and more of them by the second.

"When you left town that summer, did you know you were carrying my child?"

He tried to keep his voice hard, but she heard the pain, saw it in his eyes. "No," she swore. "No. I had no idea."

He narrowed his eyes and flexed his jaw. "Did you know you weren't coming back?"

"Of course not!" God, how could he even think that after the yearning, heated promises they'd shared when they'd said goodbye the night before she left? "I had no idea what was about to happen."

"What did happen, Beth?"

With a sigh, she rubbed her forehead. "We went to Phoenix, to my mother's cousin's, like we planned. When it was time to come home, Mother called to let Daddy know we were coming. I think…he wasn't home or something. Anyway, she ended up calling Grandma. That's when Mother found out Daddy had been…cheating on her. Apparently while we were out of town he got careless, and Grandma saw him with another woman. Mother couldn't face going home after that."

Retelling the tale made Beth's nerves stretch. She wanted to get out into the sunshine and let it burn the memories away. At the very least, she wanted to get up and pace, but there was no room in Dr. Luke Ryan's tiny office.

She folded her arms and rubbed them with her palms. "Mother didn't want anybody to know what had happened, so we left her cousin's. I thought we were going home, but she couldn't. She said she needed time to think. I tried to call you a couple of times while we were on the road, but I never got an answer. We ended up in Kansas City."

For a moment the confusion, the heartache, the sick fear that had permeated those first days and weeks in Kansas City rolled over her, threatening to steal her breath. She shook the sensation away and stared at the stark landscape on the wall over Luke's shoulder.

"Anyway, Mother and Daddy talked, and afterward she told me he…he didn't want us anymore."

"He didn't—that's crazy," Luke cried.

"I thought so, too. Mother decided to stay where she was. She was so upset, I couldn't leave her. Besides, we were out of money. I didn't have any way to get home."

"God, Beth, I would have come for you. Why didn't you call?"

Beth closed her eyes and shook her head. "I couldn't. Mother was so afraid I'd call Daddy, that I'd leave her. Every time I got near a phone she got hysterical. I didn't know what to do. Then about a week after we should have been home, I…I found out I was pregnant. Mother called to talk to Grandma about it— you know how close they've always been. That's when Grandma—oh, my God."

She stared at Luke, shock once again closing her

throat, for it was finally sinking in. "No." Her grand-mother couldn't have lied, not about something so important. There must be some other explanation. There *must* be.

"Beth?"

She shook her head. "I don't know. I need to talk to Grandma."

"No, dammit, you need to talk to me!"

Beth started at his sudden shout. "I don't know what happened," she cried. "Mother talked to Grandma, then I talked to Grandma, and some-how...somehow they told me...told me you and Carol..."

Bewildered, confused, Beth slumped in the chair. "Grandma said your picture was in the paper and everything. That you and Carol were already married by then." She raised her gaze to Luke. "There must have been...some kind of...terrible mistake."

"And she made it," Luke said with a snarl.

"No. I mean...Luke, Grandma wouldn't have lied about something like that. She couldn't. It was too important. What would be the purpose?"

"You said it yourself—it was too important, Beth. Too damn important for her to make a *mistake*."

"But...*why?*"

"How the hell do I know why Rose Shoemaker does anything? Mostly out of spite, I think. Why did she never even tell your father you had a son, for crying out loud? She told *me* you didn't want to come back to Rangely. You hadn't been gone three weeks, and she came right up to me at church and told me you were marrying some rich damn doctor."

Beth sprang from the chair. "She did not!"

"She damn sure did! She said it with a malicious grin on her face in front of at least a dozen people right smack in front of the First Baptist Church after services."

Stunned, sickened, with heat burning her cheeks and dampness coating her palms, Beth fell back to the chair again. "She lied."

"Of course she lied," Luke said heatedly. "Ask anyone in town. I've never been married."

Tears clogging her throat and blurring her vision, Beth shook her head. "Neither have I."

Lies. It was all lies. Her whole life, and Ryan's, and Luke's, and her father's, and maybe even her mother's. All built on lies. The sheer scope of the effects of her grandmother's betrayal—for Beth had no doubt now that this was her grandmother's doing, although she had no idea why—was unbelievable. How could Grandma have done such a thing? And for the love of God, *why?*

A scream built in Beth's chest.

She covered her mouth with both hands. She couldn't fall apart. Not here, not now, not in front of Luke.

The phone on his desk rang.

Beth jerked.

Luke swore. With his gaze locked on hers, he took a slow, deep breath and answered the phone on the third ring.

"Okay," he said into the receiver. "I'll be right there." He hung up. "I have a patient to see."

Beth struggled for calm. After a shaky nod, she pushed herself to her feet, hitched up her purse and headed for the door.

Luke stopped her with a hand on her arm. "Where are you going?"

"You'll need your office."

"I know, but…we need to talk, Beth. You're not leaving town, are you?"

Staring at the door before her, she said, "No. Not yet."

Luke used every ounce of control he possessed to keep his voice level, his hands steady, when what he wanted to do was smash everything in sight. Short of that, he wanted to pull Beth into his arms and never, *never* let her go again.

God, she wouldn't even look at him.

The last time he'd let her go, she'd been gone sixteen years. Not this time, by damn. Not this time.

He pulled her back to the desk and pushed a notepad and pen in front of her. "I want your address and phone number."

Startled, she jerked her gaze to his. "What for?"

"Insurance. In case your grandmother comes up with something new to send you running again."

The stricken look on her face made him swear. "I'm sorry," he said. "But I've spent sixteen years blaming you. It's…"

"It's hard to stop. I know," she said softly. Without another word she bent and wrote her address and phone number on the pad. Then she straightened and faced him again. "Whatever has happened, Luke, Ryan is innocent."

"I know that. I want a chance to know him, Beth."

She nodded. "He wants to know you, too."

"He wants to beat the crap out of me, you mean."

* * *

By the time Beth and Ryan checked in to the motel and unloaded the car, Beth thought she almost had the violent shaking under control. Ryan had questioned her the minute she'd stepped from Luke's office. She appreciated the fact that her son had let her get away with not answering.

Now he stood at the foot of the double bed nearest the door, watching her. "Mom?"

Beth sighed. She was tired. Bone-deep weary. But she had to tell him *something*. "Come sit." She held out her hand.

They sat on separate beds, facing each other. Beth took both his hands in hers. "There's been a...mistake, Ryan."

"Mistake?"

"A terrible one. I don't know how it happened, or why. Luke...your father...isn't married. Has never been married."

"What? What do you mean?"

"I mean that I kept you away from him all these years because I thought he was married, that he had other children. I was afraid he would hurt you."

"I know that."

"But he wasn't married. He doesn't have any other children. All this time I've thought he was married, and he thought I was."

Ryan stared at her, confused, hurt, bewildered. She knew exactly how he felt.

"But..."

She swallowed past the lump of tears in her throat. "I don't have any answers. I don't know how it happened, or why. I just had to tell you, so you wouldn't...go on thinking badly of him. He wants to spend some time with you, get to know you." She saw him start to speak but cut him off. "You don't have to decide right now. We're both too tired to think straight. Let's get some sleep, then we'll figure out what to do."

With the drapes pulled and the lights out, the motel room was almost as dark as night. Beth lay curled under the covers, her back to Ryan where he stretched out in the other bed. She held her breath as long as she could, then let it out, held it, let it out. The routine helped keep the tears at bay. But not for long.

Please, God, she thought as she lost the battle and the tears streamed, *don't let Ryan hear me crying.*

But he heard.

Chapter Four

A son. Dear God, he had a fifteen-year-old son.

Luke sat on his couch and stared at the grass he'd tracked across the carpet yesterday after mowing the backyard. He took another swig of beer, thanking God he was off duty for the next few days. He hadn't felt the need or desire to get falling-down drunk in years. Tonight it seemed like the thing to do. Either that or walk half a block to Rose Shoemaker's house and strangle her.

Of the two, getting drunk seemed more prudent, if less satisfying.

But beer wasn't going to do the job. Not fast enough to suit him. He got up and dug around in the back of the cabinet over the refrigerator for the bottle of bourbon Hershel Brady had given him last Christmas for not telling anyone that Luke had spent forty-five minutes Christmas Eve picking splinters out of Hershel's hairy butt. Luke had always suspected the real reason for the bourbon was for not asking how Hershel had managed to get splinters in his rear but none in his pants.

Luke rinsed out his twenty-four-ounce iced tea glass, dropped three ice cubes into it, then filled it to within an inch of the top with bourbon.

God, he thought, sinking back down onto the couch. He took a sip and shuddered as the fire burned a path down his esophagus and started eating at his stomach lining.

How in holy hell could Beth have believed he'd knocked up her best friend? How could she believe he would have married Carol?

Same way you believed she'd married some doctor.

But that was different. He hadn't believed it. Not really. But Beth hadn't come home, and her father had confirmed she wasn't going to. That added credence to Rose's lie.

Besides, neither Luke nor Leon had had any way of contacting Beth to ask if it was true, to demand an explanation. He couldn't say the same for Beth. She said she'd tried to call, but that was before she was told he was married.

Hell, she hadn't even needed to call him. She could have called anyone in town and learned the truth. But she hadn't.

Damn her.

He took another sip, this one every bit as fiery and bitter as the first. With a clank, he set the drink down on the glass-topped coffee table, then kicked off his shoes.

Damn her. Sixteen years. Lost. Wasted.

Well, not all of it was wasted, he thought with grim irony. Rose's lie did have a positive outcome. After Luke had gotten over being devastated, or as over it as he would ever get, he'd gotten mad. Leave him for some rich doctor, would she? He'd show her. He was just as good as the next man. Could be just as good a doctor as the one she'd dumped him for.

Yeah, Luke had The Old Witch and her lies to thank for his decision to enter medical school. He might have become a doctor for all the wrong reasons, but long before his internship he had realized he'd found what he wanted to do with his life.

Over the years he'd consoled himself that while he might not be as rich as the doctor Beth had married—getting rich just wasn't possible at Rangely District Hospital—he was a good doctor, and provided a much-needed service to the community. When so many small towns across America were doing without any medical help to speak of, Rangely, population 2600, had a good hospital, albeit with limited services; one of the best family clinics in existence; good doctors, of which he was one; and the best damn EMTs next door and Flight for Life units, out of St. Mary's in Grand Junction, in the country.

He'd just been extremely lucky that he hadn't been on duty the time The Old Witch had fallen on an icy sidewalk and gone in for X rays. Hell, if they'd X-rayed her chest cavity, they probably would have found a great big hole where her heart should have been.

No, maybe not a hole. A rock, probably. Or a shriveled-up prune pit. A tiny one.

Years ago Luke had given up trying to understand the bitter old woman. He couldn't for the life of him figure out how Beth could have believed her.

Damn them both. They'd cost him the first fifteen years of his son's life.

But not one more minute of it would they steal from him. Not as long as Luke lived and breathed.

After stripping off his tie and tugging his shirttail free, he stretched out on the couch and unbuttoned his collar. When he closed his eyes, it was to concentrate on how he could arrange to spend time with Ryan—Christ, she'd named their son after him. Every time he remembered that, he felt his eyes sting.

What was he like, this son of his? The brief encounter at the hospital had told Luke only two things. One, the boy, being the spitting image of his father, was a damned good-looking kid. Two, Ryan was fiercely loyal to and protective of his mother. Luke liked that. He didn't much care for the fat lip he'd gotten, but he liked the idea of his son having enough courage to take on a grown man. He just hoped the boy didn't make a habit of getting into fights.

So Luke and his son had two things in common—their looks, and strong feelings for Beth Martin. Ryan's feelings for her were obvious. Luke wasn't so sure about his own.

Her leaving had nearly killed him, but he had survived the pain, the anger, the loneliness. More than a few times over the years, her face and voice had haunted his dreams, but he'd survived.

Now she was back, and he didn't know how to feel. He'd told himself for so long that he hated her. One look into her eyes this afternoon and he'd known hate was the farthest thing from his mind. And that scared him. Terrified him, in fact.

She'd looked exhausted, now that he thought about it. Shoulders slumped, face pale, the skin around her mouth tight, circles under her eyes. But those eyes, shocked as they'd been when she'd spotted him, had still been the same soft, gray-green he remembered, had still pulled at him and made his heart thud.

Her dark brown hair, full and soft and mostly straight, still hung down to the bottoms of her shoulder blades. She still parted it on the right, still wore those wispy bangs down to her eyebrows.

The rush of conflicting emotions—love, hate, anger, longing—made him squeeze his eyes shut. Those were all old feelings for the girl he used to know. She was a woman now, thirty-four years old. A mother. A stranger.

And he wanted, more than he'd ever wanted anything in his life, for her and their son to be a part of his life. A sobering thought.

When he reached for his drink, his hand shook.

The pounding on the front door woke him. He tried to ignore it. From the cursing accompanying the pounding, he must have been somewhat successful, at least for a while.

"Sheriff's Department! Open up!"

Luke groaned. *Go away, Sheriff's Department.*

The pounding continued.

Luke groaned again, then rolled over. And ended up flat on his face on the floor between the couch and the coffee table before he realized he wasn't in his bed.

"Open up or I'm using my key!"

"Yeah, yeah," Luke grumbled to himself. "I'm coming."

Damn, he thought, pushing himself to his feet one agonizing inch at a time. His head throbbed like a sore thumb. His neck felt as if he'd slept in a vise. He'd banged one shoulder and a kneecap against the edge of the coffee table on his way to the floor. His mouth tasted as though five thousand barefoot legionnaires had marched across his tongue, and his back refused to straighten.

As he drew closer to the front door, the pounding from the other side echoed painfully behind his eyes.

"Luke!"

Luke flung open the door and glared at his brother. "What?" he snapped.

J. D. Ryan gave his younger brother a slow, narrow-eyed scrutiny. "Jeez, you look even worse than I expected."

"Good morning to you, too." Luke's voice rasped like sandpaper and felt like fire. "Sheriff's Department." Luke snorted. "You lied. You're not even in uniform. Probably woke up the whole damn neighborhood." He turned from the door and headed for the coffeepot. "Please, God, don't let me be out of coffee."

"I'll make the coffee." J.D. followed him inside and shut the door. "You don't look like you could stand up long enough. And I seriously doubt I woke up anybody but you," he said as he started filling the coffeemaker. "It's a quarter to noon."

Luke eased onto a chair at the kitchen table and swore. Beth had probably already been and gone from the hospital. Damn her, if she left town again without telling him, he'd drag her back by the hair. He wasn't finished with that woman yet. Not by a long shot.

"Must have been a hell of a night."

At the intrusion of J.D.'s voice, Luke stopped rubbing his face and peered across the kitchen to find his brother holding the nearly empty bottle of bourbon between his thumb and forefinger.

Luke grunted. "It wasn't nearly that interesting. I only had about three swallows."

"Must have been mighty big swallows." J.D. shot Luke a piercing look.

"Take it easy, Deputy. Most of what's missing from that bottle is still in the glass in the living room."

J.D. set the bottle down. "Must have been a hell of a big glass."

"It was."

The coffeemaker hissed and gurgled and dripped. The sun bounced off the glass-topped patio table just beyond the sliding glass doors next to Luke's chair and stabbed straight through his eyeballs like sharp knives. With a muffled moan, he shifted his chair around until the glare was behind him.

"So if you didn't drink all this," J.D. said, "how come you look like you've been on a three-day binge?"

Luke massaged the back of his aching neck. "Fell asleep on the damn couch."

J.D. pulled out the chair opposite Luke's and sat. "You wanna talk about it?"

"The couch? Naw. Six feet long, brown, a couple

of matching throw pillows. Same couch I've had for years.''

"Funny. How about Beth Martin? Wanna talk about her? Or maybe even her son?''

Luke dropped his hand to his lap and closed his eyes. "Word travels fast.''

"Especially when my son is on hand when you meet your son.''

"Yeah.''

J.D. got up and poured them each a cup of coffee. Luke clung to his like a lifeline.

"So," J.D. said with about as much nonchalance as a bull elephant, "what happens now?''

"I wish I knew, brother. I wish to hell I knew.''

With Ryan at her side, Beth hurried down the hospital corridor to her father's room. It was nearly noon. Had he decided she wasn't coming back?

She and Ryan had returned last night, but her father had been asleep. They'd sat quietly in his room for a few minutes, then left.

Her afternoon nap yesterday after the confrontation with Luke had left her unable to sleep last night until early morning. Then she'd overslept, and Ryan had let her. They'd grabbed a late breakfast at the Cowboy Corral on Main, then come straight to the hospital.

Breakfast had been...interesting. Kathy Elam, a classmate of Beth's, had recognized her. The reunion had been fun, at first.

"My stars! Beth Martin. Is that really you?''

For the second time in two days Beth had noted how odd it felt, seeing someone for the first time in so many years and noticing so few changes. The woman before her might as well still have been three rows over in their geometry class. A little extra weight, a few wrinkles, a tad more bleach than in high school, but no drastic differences. Beth had smiled and asked about Kathy's family. The two had chatted a moment, then Kathy's eyes had narrowed.

"I can't believe the way you ran out on Luke. He was crazy about you, and you just disappeared."

Unprepared for the venom in her former friend's voice—although after what she'd learned from Luke, she shouldn't have been—Beth had been at a loss for words.

Ryan, bless him, had slipped his arm around Beth's shoulders and said, "Hey, Mom, are you gonna introduce us?"

Kathy had given Ryan a polite smile, glared back at Beth, then, eyes popping wide, whipped back to Ryan with an astonished double take. "My stars. Well, my stars!"

While Kathy was still gaping, Mr. Bower, on his way to the cash register, had stopped at Beth's table. For as long as Beth could remember, Old Man Bower had lived next door to her parents. A full generation older than Leon and Margaret Martin, he'd always had steel gray hair and stooped shoulders. Beth had thought him ancient when she'd first met him, when she'd been a toddler. She still thought so.

He'd peered at her through thick-lensed glasses. "Leon's girl, aren't you? Been out of town? Don't recall seeing you around lately."

And what, Beth had thought, was one supposed to say to a remark like that?

Kathy Elam had choked; Ryan had blinked. Beth

had managed to smile and say, "Yes, sir. I've been out of town."

"Well," the old man had said with a firm nod, "good to have you back, girl. Tell your daddy I hope he gets well in a hurry. And you remember to keep the level down on that infernal music you always play, you hear?" Then he'd winked one blue-veined eyelid at her and walked off.

Just outside her father's room Ryan chuckled. "Did that old guy really think you'd only been on a trip?"

Beth paused and smiled. "As I remember, he always was a little...absentminded."

With both of them smiling, they stepped into the hospital room. Once again, the sight of the gray, ill man in the bed jolted against the lifelong image of her father in her mind. But he looked better today, didn't he? His eyes seemed brighter, his skin a little less gray.

By the relieved look on his face, she knew her father had been waiting for them. "There you are."

Beth took his hand and kissed his cheek. "Sorry we're so late, but we overslept."

"Did you stay at the house?"

She shook her head. "The motel."

The disappointment in his eyes brought an ache to her chest. She pushed it aside for lighter things. "We saw Mr. Bower at the Cowboy Corral just now. He said for you to hurry and get well. Does he still live next door?"

"Yeah. What did he say about you being back in town?"

Beth and Ryan shared a look, then laughed.

"What?" Leon wanted to know.

"He said he hadn't seen me around lately. Asked if I'd been on a trip."

Leon smiled a moment, then that sad, anxious look came back over his face. "Where have you been, Beth? What happened? Why didn't you come home?"

Beth lowered her gaze and fiddled with the shoulder strap of her purse, which she'd yet to put down. "What was there to come home to? You didn't want me anymore."

"Didn't want...? What are you saying? I begged your mother to come home, to bring you back. I begged."

As her head swirled, Beth felt the plain white walls close in on her. Oh, God, oh, God, not again! Not another set of lies!

She scarcely heard Ryan mumble something about getting a soda and waiting in the lobby as she sank down onto the chair beside her father's bed. Even after a heavy swallow, she still couldn't meet her father's gaze.

"Mother said...you didn't want us anymore. She said you'd found someone else. Grandma had seen you—"

The swearword that burst from her father's lips was one she'd never heard him say before. Startled, Beth looked up at him.

"I knew The Old Witch had something to do with it. I just never knew what."

"The Old Witch?"

He grunted under his breath. "A little pet name I have for your grandmother. And a hell of a lot nicer than the ones she has for me. So tell me what happened, Beth. Tell me what she said.''

She shook her head. "I don't know. I don't think I know anything anymore." She told him much of what she'd told Luke the day before about leaving Phoenix but not coming home. ''I didn't believe Mother when she said you didn't want us anymore. And in truth, Daddy, even if it had been true, there was still Luke. We were going to get married that summer. I knew I had to find a way to get home. But every time I mentioned it, Mother got hysterical. I couldn't get near the phone or the door without her falling apart. Then I realized I was pregnant, and Mother gave in. She agreed that I needed to go back to Luke.''

Beth fell silent, once again reliving that traumatic day when what was left of her world had collapsed.

''Mother called Grandma to tell her we were coming home, and why. That's when Grandma told us Luke had married Carol.''

''Good God,'' her father said with a moan. ''She lied, Beth, she lied!''

''I know. I know that now. Luke and I talked yesterday. What I don't know is why, Daddy. Why would Grandma make up something like that? It doesn't make any sense.''

He squeezed her hand. ''What are you going to do?''

''I'm going to go see her. Today. I'm going to demand some answers.''

''And then what, sweetie? Will you be going back to... Good God, I don't even know where you live.''

Beth hung her head and fought a long, silent battle

with tears. "Kansas City," she whispered. "We live in Kansas City, Mother, Ryan and I. Luke has our address and phone number."

"How long before you have to go back?"

"I don't know. Luke wants a chance to get to know Ryan."

"And how do you feel about that?"

"I'm glad. Now that I know the truth, I want Ryan to get to know his father. Ryan wants it, too, I think."

"Luke's turned into a fine man, Beth."

She smiled sadly. "I always thought he would." Then she took a deep breath to clear her head. "Is it my imagination, or do you look better today?"

"Don't know about looks, but I feel some better."

She took his hand in hers and squeezed. "I'm so glad, Daddy. I'm going to go now and let you get some rest. We'll be back later today."

"Going to your grandmother's?"

"Yes. It's time."

When Luke called the nurses' station to check Leon's condition and found out Beth was there visiting her father, he didn't allow himself a breath of relief. She was still in town, but that didn't mean she wouldn't leave any minute.

He changed clothes in record time and drove rather than walked one block up the hill to the hospital. A two-year-old forest green Oldsmobile with Missouri tags, the only car in the small lot, told him she was still here. Breathless, more from anticipation and anxiety than anything else, he jogged to the door and pulled it open.

And skidded to a halt at the sight of his son. Good

God. His *son*. Luke wondered if he would ever get used to the idea of having a nearly grown son.

The boy, Ryan, was slouched on the sofa, an ankle crossed over the opposite bouncing knee, thumbing through a copy of *Sports Illustrated*. As Luke stepped through the door, Ryan's eyes were on him—wary, cautious, yet eager. It was the eagerness that warmed something inside Luke. "Hi," he offered.

Ryan sprang to his feet. After a pause he tossed the magazine onto the coffee table and stuffed his hands into his jeans pockets. "Hi. Did you come to see my granddad?"

"Partly. I'm not on duty today, but I heard he was doing better. Thought I'd check on him. But I was hoping to catch you and your mother while you were here."

Another pause stretched as Luke waited for Ryan to say something.

"Did your mother tell you—"

"Mom told me—"

They spoke at once, stopped at once.

After a hesitation, Luke said, "So what do you think?"

Ryan gave a one-shouldered shrug. "Guess maybe I shouldn't have punched you."

Luke smiled wryly and touched the tender edge of his lip. "Wish you hadn't, but under the circumstances, I can't say I blame you."

An awkward silence followed, in which Luke and Ryan covertly studied each other. Suddenly Luke chuckled. "Does this feel as odd to you as it does to me?"

Ryan ducked his head. "Guess so." Then he

looked up and grinned. "But at least I've always known about you. I never thought I'd ever meet you, but you didn't even know I existed. Guess I was kind of a surprise, huh?"

Luke smiled back. "That's putting it mildly." Then he sobered. "The best surprise I've had in my life."

Ryan ducked his head again, but not before Luke saw the flush on his cheeks.

"What do you say we start over and do this right?" Luke asked.

Ryan raised his head, his eyes questioning.

Luke held out his hand. "Hi. I'm Luke Ryan."

Ryan swallowed. The sudden sheen of tears in his eyes was nearly Luke's undoing. But then Ryan blinked, smiled and shook Luke's hand. "Hi. I'm Ryan Martin."

And that's how Beth found them. Father and son. Shaking hands. Introducing themselves. Her heart cracked wide open. Pain and love poured out, flooding her, choking her, blurring her vision. They shouldn't have had to introduce themselves, to meet as strangers. Not a father and son. Luke was right. He should have been there with her when their son was born, and every day since.

"Mom?"

She couldn't answer.

"It's all right, Mom. I mean—isn't it?"

Nodding, lips mashed together to hold back a sob, Beth held out her arms and Ryan came to her. She hugged him tight, fighting for control of her emotions. She didn't want to cry.

From the corner of her eye she saw Luke watching them, a look of yearning on his face.

They'd missed so much, her son and his father. God, what she wouldn't give to have the years back, do them over again.

"Luke," she managed.

He met her gaze, and the need in his eyes was more than she could bear. "Luke." She reached for him, pulled him close. When his arm came around her, holding her, sheltering her against his strength, she sagged.

His other arm wrapped around Ryan's shoulders. Beth could feel the stillness of wonder come over Luke as he held his son for the first time.

She wasn't going to make it. She couldn't hold back. A sob broke loose. Then another.

"Ah, babe, don't cry," Luke whispered.

Babe. No one had called her that in sixteen years. No one but Luke had ever called her that.

"It'll be all right, babe, you'll see. It'll be all right."

Luke's own words burned in his chest. Would anything ever be all right again? How could they right the past? Nothing could make up for the time the three of them had lost. Nothing.

Ryan bent his head until it rested beside his mother's. With a sigh, Luke rested his cheek against them where their heads met. God, it felt so good. So damn good. As if his world had been tilted without his knowing and had suddenly righted itself. He held on tight to his son and the only woman he'd ever loved. The woman he feared he had never stopped loving, would never stop loving.

She trembled against him, and he held on more tightly.

Then, on a deep breath, she straightened and dabbed at her eyes. "Daddy seems better today." She stepped back.

Luke let his arm slide from her shoulder, acutely feeling the loss of her warmth. "So I heard." His voice came out surprisingly even. "I came to see for myself."

"Is he going to be okay?" Gray-green eyes, more gray than green just then and still watery, beseeched him. "Is he going to get well?"

"I won't kid you, Beth. When he asked me to have your grandmother find you he was as sick as I've ever seen anyone. We were doing everything we could, but it wasn't enough. He needed a reason to get well. Looks like you might have given him one by coming back. I think he's got a chance now. A good chance."

"His color looked better today," she said anxiously.

"That's good. I'm going to go check on him. But I had another reason for coming. I told Ryan I'd hoped to catch the two of you. Since Mike was here yesterday, you can imagine the word is out."

"More than you think," Beth told him. "We ran into Kathy Elam at breakfast. She took one look at Ryan and—"

Luke stiffened. "What'd she say?"

"I believe her exact words were 'My stars.'"

"You don't seem to be upset about it. Neither of you," he added, noticing Ryan's grin.

Beth cast Ryan a glance, then met Luke's gaze. "We're not if you're not."

"You know there are no secrets in this town," he reminded her. "Everyone knows everyone else's business. If that weren't enough," he told his son, "we Ryan men all look like clones. People will remember your mother and I used to go together. They'll know who you are."

Ryan cocked his head. "Yeah? So?"

"I don't want you hurt because of something that's not your fault. I don't know how long you're planning on staying in town, but—"

"You don't think the talk will get ugly, do you?" Beth asked.

"No." Luke grinned wryly. "Not ugly. But there's going to be a lot of ribbing."

Ryan put his arm back around Beth's shoulders and looked at Luke with a half smile. "We don't care if you don't."

Luke let out the breath he hadn't realized he'd been holding. "Good, then. The rest of the family wants to see you, Beth, and they want to meet Ryan. I'd like to take the two of you out to the ranch for dinner tonight. Dad's gonna grill steaks."

"Your father…"

Luke saw her uncertainty, felt it. He understood the way she gripped Ryan's shoulder. It was a protective measure, maternal, instinctive, to keep her son from harm.

"They've already heard the two of you are here. They're anxious to see you. It's just family, Beth."

Still, she hesitated.

"Please."

Chapter Five

Luke was going to pick them up at the motel at five.

Beth hadn't been sure accepting the invitation had been the best thing to do, until she'd seen the look on Ryan's face. She'd been worried about his having to deal with too much too soon. And truth to tell, she'd been just as worried about her own ability to handle all that was happening. But one look at the eagerness in Ryan's eyes and she'd had no choice but to accept.

However, before the sun set on another day, Beth intended to have some answers.

After much protesting on Ryan's part, Beth left her son in their motel room and headed to her grandmother's. This was one scene she didn't want him to witness. Beth had the sickening feeling things were going to get extremely unpleasant. Her grandmother would not want to answer questions, and would probably deny any accusations Beth threw at her.

But Beth would not be put off. Not after all she'd learned in the past two days. She had too much anger in her, too much outrage, too much pain and confusion.

Less than five minutes after leaving Ryan at the motel, Beth stood at her grandmother's front door and rang the bell. She hadn't finished wiping her palms on her slacks when the door opened.

Rose Shoemaker hadn't aged well. Every one of her sixty-seven years was etched around her eyes and perpetually frowning mouth, down her sunken cheeks, across her narrow brow, in deep, harsh lines emphasized by the application of too much foundation makeup, too much rouge. Behind the lenses of her jewel-framed glasses her gray eyes looked faded and washed out below startling blue eye shadow.

"Bethany!" The pale gray eyes blinked slowly.

A sudden calm settled inside Beth. The fear and dread of confrontation disappeared, as did the nervous fluttering in her stomach. This was no unknown monster, merely the grandmother she'd known all her life. No horns or fangs, just an old woman.

Grandma hadn't changed in the past two days. The lies she had used to alter lives had been concocted years ago. All that had changed was Beth's knowledge of what was inside the woman. No more blinders for Beth. No more seeing only what she wanted to see. She straightened her shoulders and met her grandmother's startled gaze. "Hello, Grandma. You look surprised to see me."

Surprised wasn't an accurate description for the

look on her grandmother's face. Put out was more like it. Aggravated. Not one hint of concern that her lies might be discovered.

"Well, I must say I am surprised. What does your mother think? Where is she?"

"She's still on vacation. Are you going to invite me in?"

"Don't be impertinent, dear. Of course I'm going to invite you in." She stepped back from the door and motioned Beth inside.

Dark. Grandma's house was always so dark. Every window was covered in heavy, lined drapes pulled tight to keep out even a hint of the outside world. Except in the living room. Beth barely glanced at the furnishings, other than to note they were new. She went straight to the huge picture window overlooking the entire town, the entire basin. Shades and layers of whites and grays, greens and browns and blues.

The sight took her breath away. God, but she'd missed it. All of it. The trees and grass planted in town, the stark desert surrounding it, the bluff just across the river. Blue Mountain rising in the distance. Even the oil wells looked good to her, what few there were left since the bust back in the eighties. She had never realized just how much she had loved this town, this country, until right that moment. What she wouldn't give to be able to look out this window every day for the rest of her life.

She might have done so—not from this window, but a similar one somewhere in town—but for the woman standing just behind her shoulder. But for her own grandmother, who'd stolen it all away with her lies.

"You made good time," Rose said.

"Better than you think." Beth tore herself from the view and faced her grandmother. "We got here yesterday."

Rose blinked, startled. "Yesterday? We? You said—"

"Ryan came with me."

Rose's chin jerked. "That was most unwise, don't you think?"

"Why is that, Grandma? What's wrong with letting my son see the town I grew up in?"

"Use your head, Bethany, for once."

"No, Grandma, you use yours. Let's cut this out, shall we?"

"I won't have that kind of talk from you, young lady."

Beth smiled bitterly. "All right, I'll speak very nicely when I ask you the questions I have to ask you."

"What questions?"

Rigid. From her voice to her eyes to the way she held her head and shoulders, the very way she lived her life and tried to run the lives of others, Rose Shoemaker was a rigid person. Beth had always known that, had always accepted it.

No longer. Beth accepted nothing anymore at face value. She leveled her gaze on the woman before her. "Tell me what would happen if I walked down the street and asked the first person I came to if Luke Ryan had ever been married."

Beneath the makeup and rouge, Rose paled.

"If I went down to the paper and looked through sixteen-year-old issues of *The Rangely Times,* who would be standing next to Carol Thompson in her wedding picture, Grandma, Luke Ryan or Jerry Howard?''

After a moment of heavy silence, Rose unpursed her lips. "Well, I can see your questions are rhetorical. Sit down, dear, and I'll brew a pot of tea."

"Tea?" Beth shrieked. "I don't want tea, I want answers!"

Rose jerked again. "I will not be talked to this way."

"You manipulate my life, my son's life, Luke's life, maybe even Mother and Daddy's lives, deny my son his father for *fifteen years,* and you *won't be talked to this way?*"

With her head erect, Rose walked sedately past Beth and entered the kitchen. "Don't be melodramatic, dear. It's so unbecoming."

"Don't you dare patronize me." Beth shook with sheer rage. "You're not even denying all the lies, are you?"

With astounding calm, Rose filled the teakettle with water, placed it on the stove and bent slightly to turn on the gas burner beneath it. When she straightened and met Beth's gaze with total composure, Beth wanted to scream.

"I did what was necessary for your best interest and your mother's. And look how well everything turned out. You have a good career, a fine son, a beautiful home in a lovely city. Had I not stepped in, you would have none of those things. And look at Luke," she said, one penciled-in eyebrow arching. "He's a good doctor, well respected in the community. If you had stayed and the two of you had married that summer, he would never have had the opportunity to attend medical school. What I did was for the best, dear. If you think about it rationally, I'm sure you'll agree.''

Dazed by her grandmother's twisted justifications, Beth could do no more than stare for long moments. Then she said, ''Grandma, doesn't it matter to you that I haven't been really happy since the day I left town?''

''That's nonsense, and you know it. You've been perfectly fine. How happy do you think you would have been stuck out on that sheep ranch for the past sixteen years with a passel of Ryan brats hanging on your skirts?''

''It's all I ever wanted, Grandma.''

''You think I don't know that? I've always known he was what you wanted. That's why I did what I did—for your sake.''

Beth didn't know whether to cry or scream or break something. Not one single ounce of remorse did she see in her grandmother's eyes. No guilt, not even chagrin at being caught in her lies. Nothing but solid conviction that she'd done the right thing.

But it hadn't been right. Not for Beth, not for any of them. Beth ground her teeth, incensed at the pain and destruction the woman before her had caused.

''It's done now, Grandma, and can't be undone. But be warned, your lies and your manipulation will no longer be tolerated. By any of us. When the story gets out, everyone in town is going to know what you've done.''

''What are you talking about?''

Aha. Finally, a reaction. Beth knew full well how

much her grandmother concerned herself with the opinions of others.

"No one's going to know a thing," Rose stated, a slight quiver in her voice.

"You don't think for a minute that anyone could look at Ryan and not know who his father is, do you?"

"What are you doing, parading your son up and down Main Street?"

"No, but I'm not hiding him, either. Whatever game you've been playing is over, Grandma. Over. I will never, *never* allow you to hurt any of us again."

Beth was still shaking from the encounter with her grandmother when she pulled in to the motel parking lot nearly an hour later. She'd done her best to hide her agitation from her father when she'd visited him, but she wasn't sure how successful she'd been. He had urged her to stay in his house rather than the motel. Because it seemed to mean so much to him, she agreed to think about it. She'd been grateful that he hadn't pressed her for answers she didn't have.

One question kept prodding her. Had her mother known about the lies? Had she been in on the whole thing? Was it all some bizarre conspiracy to tear Beth and Luke apart?

Beth shook her head. "I'm getting paranoid."

Lord, what was she supposed to do with all these emotions? Pain and rage, betrayal, frustration and an overwhelming sense of loss all boiled together inside her, seeking a way out, ready to erupt. And all she could do was clamp down on them and hope they didn't boil over.

Then there was the question of what to tell Ryan.

She was spared from that dilemma for the time being, but only because another problem presented itself. Just as she got out of her car, a burgundy Lincoln Mark VII pulled in to the spot next to her. Behind the wheel sat Luke.

Panicked, Beth glanced at her watch. Surely he was way too early to take them to the ranch.

But he wasn't.

Ryan stepped out of the motel room to greet her.

"Give me five minutes to freshen up," she told them as she slipped past Ryan and into the room.

As good as her word—Beth wasn't one to fuss over her appearance—she rejoined the men in just under five minutes. They piled into Luke's car, Ryan beating Beth into the back seat, and headed east out of town.

"Nice car," Ryan commented.

"Thanks." Luke ran a hand along the console between the front bucket seats. "I've only had it a few months."

The soft hum of the powerful engine and the higher-pitched singing of tires on pavement filled the silence that followed the brief exchange. Beth bit the inside of her cheek, fighting that boiling pot of emotions again. Her son and his father were reduced to awkward comments, like the strangers they were.

"Who will we see at the ranch?" she asked, to fill the silence.

A look of relief crossed Luke's face before he was able to hide it. "Dad'll be there, of course. That's your grandfather," he said to Ryan's reflection in the rearview mirror. "You met your cousin Mike. His sister, Sandy, will be there. She's sixteen. And their dad, your uncle, J.D.'' Luke tossed Beth a smirk. ''J.D.'s a deputy sheriff.''

Beth blinked. ''You're kidding, right?''

Luke grinned. ''Nope. It's a fact.''

Beth shook her head, fighting a grin. ''He can't be. Not the J. D. Ryan I remember. The one who set off those firecrackers under old Mr. Higgins's desk in English, while Mr. Higgins was sitting there? The one who used to pull all the fire alarms so we could get out of class? The one who drilled that peephole in the wall of the girls' locker room?''

''One and the same,'' Luke swore.

''Your uncle J.D.,'' she told Ryan over her shoulder, ''was always in trouble.''

''He's even got himself a new wife,'' Luke offered.

''What,'' Beth asked, ''did he do with the old one?''

Luke chuckled. ''Maureen took off years ago. Left him and the kids, saying she couldn't stand it here another day. This past winter he married Mike and Sandy's history teacher. Name's Kat. She'll be there, too.''

As Luke slowed to turn up Douglas Creek, Beth fell silent again, her attention snared by the familiar terrain. Bare rocky ground, sagebrush, sticker bushes that next fall would turn into genuine tumbleweeds.

''You don't have to worry about making explanations,'' he said softly. ''I've already told them what your grandmother did.''

If he'd meant to relieve her, it didn't work. Beth's nerves stretched tighter.

Luke turned up East Douglas Creek, and soon Beth

recognized the Ryan ranch ahead. Again, as with the town, she was surprised. The ranch wasn't tiny and run-down. The big white house looked as if it wore a fresh coat of paint. Barn, garage and sheds all looked in good repair.

By the time Luke parked next to the house, Beth was a bundle of nerves. Standing on the gravel next to the car, she wanted to link her arm through Ryan's for support. For both of them. But she could see the tension gripping her son, heard it fairly humming in the air between them.

And Ryan *was* tense. He felt the sweat on his palms and surreptitiously wiped it off on his jeans. People were coming out of the house. His family.

Until this trip to Colorado, he'd had his mom, his grandmother and his great-grandmother. He glanced quickly to the man rounding the front of the car to stand beside his mother. Ryan swallowed. Now he had…God, he had a father.

And it didn't stop there. Back at the hospital he had a grandfather. Now here was another one, plus two cousins and an aunt and uncle. What if…what if they didn't like him?

He glanced at his father again.

But Luke was watching Beth. Standing beside her, he saw her uncertainty as the family spilled out the front door onto the porch, saw that uncertainty magnified a hundredfold on Ryan's face. Luke wanted to do something, say something to ease their tension.

J.D. beat him to it. With a whoop and a holler he jumped off the porch and caught Beth up in a big bear hug. "Hot damn, look at you! All grown up and prettier than ever, and boy, are we glad to see you."

Zach came next. "Unhand that girl before you break her in two." He tugged on J.D.'s arm until Beth was once again standing on her feet, this time wearing a watery grin. "As head of this family," Zach said solemnly, "I should have gotten to go first."

Then with damp eyes and gentle hands, Zach pulled Beth into his arms. "Welcome home, honey. Welcome home."

"Mr. Ryan," Beth mumbled against his chest.

"Zach, honey. You call me Zach."

While Zach closed his eyes and laid his cheek against the top of Beth's head, J.D. held a hand out to Ryan. "You're Ryan. The name suits you." He gave a sharp nod. "I'm your uncle. J.D. Welcome to the family." Then J.D. grinned. "I've never had a nephew before."

Ryan shook hands and gave back a shaky grin. "I've never had an uncle before."

Any tension remaining eased as everyone laughed at Ryan's answer. Then Zach turned Beth loose and shoved J.D. aside. "There you go again, gettin' in my way." He studied Ryan hard, his eyes misting. "Well." He cleared his throat, then cleared it again. "Ryan, is it? You do the name proud. A right fine-lookin' young man, yes, sir."

Ryan blushed.

Beth chuckled. "Yeah, he looks like you, doesn't he?"

"That's what I said. Right fine-lookin'."

"Heaven help us." J.D.'s wife—his pregnant wife—greeted Beth. "They'll all be impossible to live with now. I'm Kat, and I'm really glad to meet you."

Zach finished all the introductions, then with one

arm around Beth, the other around Ryan, he led the way to the house. The sudden emptiness in Luke's gut made him envy his father.

Beth leaned back on the couch with a sigh. "I don't think I could eat another bite." The smell of charcoal drifted through the open window from the backyard. She could still taste the steaks, baked beans, potato salad and crisp dill pickles, even over the bowl of homemade strawberry ice cream she'd devoured after the meal.

Talk had been smooth and easy all evening. Beth couldn't believe the way everyone seemed to accept Ryan and her into their midst as part of the family. Oh, she'd had no doubt they would welcome Ryan, but she hadn't anticipated them making her feel as though she belonged. It was a bittersweet feeling, knowing what she'd missed over the years. She and Ryan both.

When Mike invited Ryan to spend the night, Beth saw the silent plea in her son's eyes. The rest of the family, except Luke, added their pleas. She gave in gracefully. When they invited her, too, she declined.

Through it all, Luke watched and listened. And felt.

He watched his family absorb his son—God, he still wasn't used to that term—into the fold as though he'd always been there. They tried the same with Beth, but she was holding back slightly.

He listened to the easy banter and laughter floating around him. The teasing family jokes, sibling rivalry between Mike and Sandy, dire predictions as to how closely Kat's walk would resemble that of a duck as her pregnancy advanced. He listened to Beth answer questions about where she'd lived all these years, what she did for a living. Easy, tactful questions rather than probing ones. They all thought it was ironic that Beth worked as an office manager for a group of doctors at a clinic, while Luke himself was a doctor and spent most of his time in the clinic attached to the hospital.

He felt the empty place in his heart where memories of Beth, pregnant with their son, should have been. Memories of feeling a baby—*his* baby—kick his mother's stomach from the inside out. Memories of middle-of-the-night back rubs for a woman laboring to bring new life into the world. Memories of a birth, a man and woman raising their son together.

The hole where those memories should have been grew larger with each passing moment.

The sleek Mark VII slipped through the night as Luke drove Beth back to town. The highway was deserted beneath a star-studded sky.

"He's a terrific kid, Beth," Luke offered. "You've done a good job raising him."

"Thank you."

He shot her a glance, trying to judge her reaction to what he planned to say. She looked exhausted. He should probably wait for a better time, but he might never get her alone again. "I want some time with him. Want to get to know him."

"He'd like that."

"How much time do I have? How long are you staying?"

Beth shook her head. "I don't know. When we

came here, I only planned to see Daddy, then go home. I didn't plan on running into you."

That stung. "Because you didn't want to?"

"Because I was told years ago that you'd moved away."

Luke swore. "I guess you talked to Rose today?"

"For all the good it did me."

"What did she have to say?"

Beth gave a harsh laugh. "She said everything turned out for the best. I have a great life, and so do you. To hear her tell it, if it weren't for her, you'd still have me barefoot and pregnant out on the ranch, and you and I would both be miserable."

He swore again. "I've seen you barefoot a hundred times. If you were going to be pregnant with my child, I damn sure would have liked the chance to be around." He slammed a fist against the steering wheel. "Damn, Beth, why didn't you call and ask me if it was true? How could you even begin to believe her lies?"

Beth stared out the side window at the darkness, unable to face him. "I didn't want to believe her, but I was young and scared. My parents' marriage was falling apart before my eyes, my mother was practically hysterical, and both she and Grandma told me Daddy didn't want anything more to do with me. Everything else in my life was falling apart. It didn't seem all that surprising to have my last hope destroyed just then. I'd never known Grandma to lie. I had no reason to doubt her."

"No reason?" Luke yelled. "You knew I loved you. How could you possibly believe I would betray you with your best friend? You knew I wasn't seeing anyone but you. You knew Carol was going with Jerry. In fact, Carol *was* pregnant—with Jerry's child. She married him, is still married to him, and they have four kids. She's never forgiven you for disappearing the way you did. She's going to be really thrilled to learn you had so little faith in her as to think she'd sleep with me.''

"You think I don't know that?'' Beth cried. "You think I haven't been blaming myself every minute since you and I talked for being so stupid and gullible? But it's done, Luke. My grandmother lied, maybe my mother, too. I believed them, and because of that, I've spent the last fifteen years raising our son alone, he's spent his entire life with no father, and you've spent all these years not even knowing he existed. If there's a way to undo that, you tell me what it is, and I'll do it.''

"Don't I wish it could be undone.'' Luke turned onto Highway 64 and drove into town. "We both know it can't be. But I want to get to know my son. I want some time with him.''

Beth stared at the buildings on Main, her eyes wide and blinking to keep the tears from falling. Lord, she was losing it. When had she become so self-centered? She actually felt a stab of jealousy, and a bigger one of pain, that Luke didn't seem interested in spending any time with *her*.

"How much time are you talking about?'' she managed.

"Well, since I can't get back the last fifteen years—''

"Stop it.''

Luke sighed. At the corner lot where the old movie

theater once stood, he turned off Main and into the motel parking lot. He pulled in next to Beth's car and cut the engine. "I'm sorry. You're right. It's done, and we need to decide where and how we go on from here. But dammit, Beth, I feel like we've—like *I've*—missed so much."

He kept his hands on the steering wheel and stared at the number on the motel door just past the hood of his car. "I never got to see you swell with my child, never got to feel him kick from inside your womb. I wasn't there for you while you carried him, or when he was born. I never got to see you nurse him." He closed his eyes and swallowed. "Did you breastfeed him?"

The longing and pain in his voice matched the ache in Beth's heart. "Yes," she whispered.

Luke's throat worked on another swallow. "I never got to see him crawl, or take his first steps. I wasn't there for his first day of school, his first ball game.... And you...you had to go through all those things alone, thinking I'd betrayed you."

His emotions and hers seemed to suck all the air out of the car. Beth opened the door and got out.

Luke followed. She faced the door to her room and fumbled in her purse for the key.

"I want to know my son."

"I want that, too."

With a hand on her shoulder, he turned her toward him.

The sight of her tears twisted something inside Luke. Slowly, carefully, afraid she'd bolt if he moved too fast, he pulled her into his arms. When she didn't object, he let out his breath and rested his chin on the top of her head. "Don't cry, Beth, please. I don't want to make you cry." He turned his head and rubbed his cheek against her silky hair. "We'll work it out."

Then somehow, without conscious thought, he found himself sipping the tears from her cheeks. From there it seemed only natural to taste her eyelids, her smooth brow, down to her jaw and over to that dainty chin. She smelled of spring flowers and sunshine, with the barest hint of smoke from their cookout in her hair. Her skin was incredibly soft.

The instant his lips touched hers, she stiffened in his arms. He whispered her name, and even to his own ears, it sounded like a plea. He brushed his lips across hers again. And again. The third time, her lips moved beneath his. He was lost.

He kissed her then, full and hard, starved for the taste of her on his tongue, the feel of her beneath his hands. God, it was still there. After all the years, the old hunger was as strong as ever, for her, only for her, the fire just as hot—hotter. The kiss was both familiar and new. As familiar as the dreams that had haunted his darkest nights, as new as the taste of the woman, when before, she had been a girl.

He thought fleetingly that this woman in his arms must have a dozen men back in Kansas City standing in line begging for her favors. The thought twisted inside him like a sharp knife, but he shoved it away and deepened the kiss. This wasn't Kansas City. This was here and now, and she was in his arms. She was kissing him back, stealing his breath, making his knees quiver, his blood race.

The need for air finally pulled them apart. Under

the glow of the nearby street lamp they stared at each other, stunned, shaken.

Beth backed away, her eyes wide, lips wet and swollen from the pressure of his. "I have to go in."

"Beth—"

"Good night, Luke."

She left him standing there on the sidewalk. He squeezed his eyes shut and forced a deep, calming breath before turning back to his car.

All these years, he'd been so certain he was over her.

All these years, he'd been wrong.

Chapter Six

Something was wrong. Margaret Martin née Shoemaker stared at the phone beside the bed in her Branson hotel room and willed it to ring.

It didn't.

It wasn't like Beth not to return a call. It wasn't like her to be away from home two nights in a row, either, yet every time Margaret had called home, all she'd gotten was that blessed answering machine.

She checked her watch. Ten o'clock. Maybe Beth would call yet tonight.

Margaret fell asleep waiting for the phone to ring. It never did.

By the next morning she was fighting panic. Something was definitely wrong. She could feel it. With trembling fingers she punched in the numbers for the clinic where Beth worked, only to be told a moment later that Beth was taking a few days off.

"This is her mother," Margaret said. "I'm out of town on vacation, and I was supposed to let her know where I was staying."

"Oh, hi, Mrs. Martin. This is Maryjo."

Maryjo, Margaret knew, was the wife of one of the clinic's doctors. She didn't normally work there.

"I'm filling in for Beth while she's gone. She said there was some sort of family emergency."

"Ryan?" Margaret asked, her stomach knotting with dread. "Has something happened to Ryan?"

"No, no. I remember her saying Ryan was going with her. They were headed out of town. I'm sorry I can't be more helpful."

Mother, Margaret thought as she hung up the phone. "Something's happened to Mother."

She placed the call to Rangely immediately. At the sound of her mother's voice, Margaret's knees went weak with relief. "Mother, are you all right?"

"Of course I am."

Alarm raced through Margaret. If her mother was fine, then... "Have you heard from Beth?"

"Now, Margaret, don't get excited. This is nothing I can't handle."

"What? I haven't been able to reach her on the phone, and at the clinic they say she's out of town for some kind of family emergency. Are you sure you're all right? Where is she?"

"She's here, dear."

"There? At your house? What for?"

"Well, not at my house, but she's in town. I wish

she would have stayed home. She's making such a fuss.''

"Mother!'' Margaret took a deep breath and forced herself to stop stretching the phone cord. ''Tell me what's going on.''

Over the phone line her mother sighed. ''It's Leon. He was—is—very ill, and was asking for Beth. His doctor was concerned enough to talk to me about it, and suggested that I call Beth. The doctor seemed to think Leon was…giving up. He wasn't getting well.''

Margaret sat down heavily on the bedside. ''What…'' She had to stop and moisten her mouth before she could go on. ''What's wrong with him?''

''Pneumonia. His second or third case this year, the way I understand it.''

''So you called Beth and told her to come.''

''I most certainly did not. I called her, yes. But when I found out you weren't there, I told her to wait and discuss the situation with you. The next thing I knew, she was here. She didn't even have the courtesy to let me know she was in town until the day after she arrived.''

''I'm not sure how long it will take me to get there. I'm with friends—''

''Get here? There's no need, dear. You just go on and finish your vacation. Have a good time. I can take care of whatever problems arise here.''

''But, Mother, if Leon is ill enough that you felt the need to call, I think I should come.''

''And I think you should not. To be perfectly frank, dear, he did not ask for you. He only asked for Bethany.''

It was ridiculous. Leon's not asking for Margaret

from his sickbed should have had no effect whatsoever on her. Most especially, it should not hurt. The man had dumped her for a bleached floozy.

"Don't worry about a thing," Rose was saying. "Just have a good time on your vacation. When you get home, you can call and tell me all about it."

After hanging up the phone, Margaret sat still and stared at it. Have a good time? Her mother decreed, therefore Margaret was expected to comply. Margaret Shoemaker had always done what her mother told her. Right up to and including leaving her husband. She always gave in to her mother. Always.

Except for that one time, that one night of independence in the back seat of Leon Martin's '57 Chevy. In the dark beside an oil well that chugged and pumped so loudly that it drowned out all other sounds except the heavy breathing and desperate words of love. Amid scattered clothing, tangled arms and legs, sweat-slicked skin and fogged windows, Margaret had defied her mother's wishes. That night, two sixteen-year-olds in the desperate grip of unleashed hormones, young love and a full moon, Margaret Shoemaker and Leon Martin created their daughter.

Margaret shook her head and rose to pace the smooth gray carpet beside the bed. There was no use remembering. Not now.

Oh, how she had loved Leon, loved him with everything she had. But she'd ruined it so many years ago, long before she'd actually left him. During the past sixteen years Margaret had had plenty of time to reflect, and she'd come to the conclusion that the collapse of her marriage had started the day Beth was born.

Not through any fault of Beth's, of course. She'd been the sweetest baby, and so precious.

But with her birth had come Rose's determination to break the cycle. She had declared that Bethany Martin would not become the third generation of women in their family to end up pregnant, married and stuck in Rangely-the-Armpit-of-the-World, Colorado, for the rest of her life. Beth would not be trapped the way Rose had been, and Margaret.

Funny, but Margaret had never felt trapped, except when her mother reminded her she was.

Margaret squeezed her eyes shut. Oh, to go back and do it all again. But then, no, nothing would have been different. Not unless God saw fit to give her a backbone the second time around. And a brain in her head so she could think for herself. She could look back and see it all so clearly now, the mistakes, the way she'd allowed her mother to manipulate and brainwash her.

Hindsight was always sharp and clear. Twenty-twenty.

She'd been so stupid to let it go so far as to actually believe she was unhappy, that Leon wasn't good enough for her, that she hated Rangely. That taking Beth and leaving Leon was the thing to do, the way to break the cycle her mother had harped on for years.

Of course, Margaret thought with a smile, by the time she and Beth had left town, it was already too late. Beth had already been pregnant. That discovery, and Beth's pleading to go home, had opened Margaret's eyes. But that, too, had come too late. Leon had already found another woman, and Luke Ryan had married Beth's best friend.

Lord above, those had been rough days. The end of Beth's dreams, the end of Margaret's marriage.

Yes, if she had it to do over again, she would stick by Leon and give him back all the love he'd given her over the years.

Now he was sick. Sick enough that her mother had felt the need to call. Was he dying? Was the single love of her life wasting away in some hospital bed thinking she had never loved him?

According to her mother, Margaret was supposed to go on about her business, have a wonderful vacation and not worry about a thing. Why should Margaret worry about Leon? After all, she hadn't so much as spoken to him in sixteen years.

Well, sixteen years come next Thursday. At 10:42 p.m. Central Daylight Time.

Sixteen years. From down the hall Luke watched Ryan and Beth enter Leon's room. At fifteen, the boy was half a head taller than his mother. Luke's gaze zeroed in on Beth. Dark, glossy hair brushed her shoulder blades. Her hips swayed in a gentle female rhythm that raised his blood pressure.

Luke wanted, desperately, to call back the last sixteen years. Wanted to find a way to keep her from taking that ill-fated vacation and leaving him, wanted to strangle Rose Shoemaker so her lies couldn't destroy the future he and Beth had planned, so he wouldn't have missed the first fifteen years of his son's life.

With a shake of his head, he turned and went into

his office. He'd been right to go to Rose about calling Beth, and more than for his own benefit. After only a few days, Leon's condition had dramatically improved. He wasn't well yet, by any means, but he was getting better. Thank God.

Now, if Luke could just do something about the paperwork on his desk, he, too, would feel better. Deb Conners had picked a hell of a time to run off and get married. What was a clinic supposed to do without an office manager? She couldn't have picked someone local, so she could come back to work after the elopement. No, not Deb. Had to go and fall for some guy from Salt Lake.

And Carlos had to pick this week to come down with something contagious. This was supposed to be Luke's week off, but here he was, seeing to Carlos's patients. Except for Mrs. Murphy, Luke thought with a chuckle. She'd come in for her appointment this morning, but when she heard Dr. Carlos O'Grady was out sick, she experienced a remarkable recovery. Luke should have expected as much. Mrs. Murphy never let anyone but Carlos touch her. And as far as Luke could tell, Carlos had yet to touch her the way she wanted. So she kept coming back.

Luke shook his head. He had more important things he'd rather think about than a screwed-up appointment schedule and fellow doctors who had the nerve to get the flu. He needed to decide how he felt about Beth. What the devil was he going to do about his attraction to her? He'd been a fool to think it had actually died. That kiss the other night had proved that much. If he closed his eyes, he could still taste her lips, smell her soft floral fragrance, feel her shape beneath his hands, the way her body trembled against his.

She had been as affected as he. Her breath had been as ragged. Fitting the key into the lock on her door had taken her three tries.

But what if it had been only the moment for her, only the kiss, when for him, it had been so much more? What if all she'd felt had been nostalgia? What if she had a man waiting for her back in Kansas City?

He would drive himself crazy with "what ifs." Especially that last one.

He turned to the stack of patient folders on his desk. When the phone rang he was relieved to be interrupted, and felt guilty for feeling relieved. It was Connie calling from the nurses' station down the hall.

"What's all that commotion in the background?" he asked.

"That's why I'm calling. I think you better get down here to Mr. Martin's room in a hurry."

Luke dropped the phone and bolted from his office. Even from there he could hear the yelling. What the hell?

"You!" Leon shouted.

Shouted? Since when did Leon have the breath to shout?

"Look at you," came an irate female voice. "You don't look like you're dying to me."

"Mother!" Beth's outraged voice echoed down the hall.

Luke rounded the corner into Leon's room and skidded to a halt. He would have recognized Margaret Martin anywhere. He closed the door silently behind him to contain the loud voices in the room.

"Well," the woman said to Beth, "Mother told me he was on his deathbed, and I can see he isn't. This was just an elaborate trick of his to get me back."

Luke's first instinct was to clear the room. He didn't like confrontations around his patients. True, Leon had improved in the past few days since Beth's arrival, but he was a long way from recovered.

Yet as Luke studied Leon, saw the fire in the man's eyes, the energy—adrenaline, probably—with which he pushed himself up on one elbow, Luke swallowed the order he'd been about to issue. Leon hadn't looked this alive in years.

"Get you back?" Leon crowed. "The hell, you say. Anybody around here says they heard me ask for you, I'll kiss their a—"

"Daddy, shame," Beth scolded.

"Isn't that just like you?" Margaret said to Leon. "Toss your wife and daughter out for some cheap bimbo, and all these years later you're still throwing my feelings in my face."

"Feelings?" Leon cried. "When did you ever have any feelings? And just what was that bit about *me* tossing *you* out? Way I remember it, *wife,* you took off on vacation and never came back."

"That's because, *husband,* from the minute we left town you were seen—repeatedly—with that Della Carmichael from over at the trailer park."

"By who, by God?"

"By my mother!"

Leon eased himself back down on the bed. "Your mother." He shot a glance at Beth, then Luke, before turning his heated gaze back to Margaret. "That the same mother that told you Luke got married to Beth's best friend?''

"I've only got one mother."

"Yeah, and we'd all have been better off without her.''

"You," Margaret said between clenched teeth. "I knew I should have divorced you years ago."

"What?" Beth jumped to her feet. "What are you saying? The two of you did divorce years ago."

From the bed, Leon let out a snort. "Not hardly. Thing I want to know is, why you never filed," he said to Margaret.

"Why didn't you?"

The two glared at each other, gazes locked, lips sealed tight against revealing too much.

Finally Leon broke the spell. He tossed an arm across his eyes and let out a ragged breath. "Because, fool that I've always been for you, I thought maybe…maybe when you'd worked some of The Old Witch's poison out of your system, maybe you'd…come home. There was no other woman, Margaret. Not ever."

With a strangled cry, Margaret put a hand to her mouth and whirled toward the door. She didn't give Luke so much as a glance before fleeing.

A long moment of stunned silence filled the room before Beth finally spoke. "Daddy?"

"Della Carmichael," he said with disgust. "The Old Witch strikes again."

Luke took Leon's pulse and found it a little faster than he preferred, but not bad, under the circumstances. "I'd like you to rest now," Luke told him.

"I'll go," Beth said.

Leon pulled his arm from across his eyes and pierced her with a steady look. "I never cheated on your mother."

Beth nodded. She believed him. She rose from her chair and stood beside his bed. "I'm going to go catch up with her. I want to be there when she talks to Grandma."

"Now, there's a pleasant thought. Both of them at once. Tweedle Dumb and Tweedle Dumber. So help me, if your mother listens to one more lie from that woman, I'll wring both their necks."

Beth leaned down and kissed his cheek. "Don't worry, I'll handle it. You just rest."

He and Luke watched her go.

Leon threw his arm over his eyes again. "If they leave me again, Luke, you can just go right on out and bury me, so help me God, you can."

Beth caught up with her mother at her grandmother's front door.

"I don't believe him," Margaret said hotly. "I don't believe for a minute he wasn't seeing another woman."

"Mother." Beth felt pain well up in her chest. She touched her mother's arm. "Before you talk to Grandma, there are some things you need to know."

Chapter Seven

Leon was sleeping when Luke went off duty that evening.

Carlos had called as Luke was leaving, swearing he was over the flu and would be back at work the next day. Between the rest of Luke's week off and the days Carlos would work for him as payback, Luke had the next seven days free. He intended to spend as much time as possible with his son. And his son's mother.

To that end, he went looking for them. Beth's car wasn't at her grandmother's, so he figured that particular confrontation between the three women was over with for the time being. God, what a mess. He drove past Rose's street and headed for the motel.

When he pulled in the parking lot, his heart dropped into his stomach. Beth's car was there, all right, the green Olds with Missouri tags. Beth was there, too. Stowing a suitcase in the trunk.

He couldn't believe it. Damn her, was she sneaking out on him again? How long would she stay gone this time—twenty years? Thirty? Was she going to rip him to pieces again, this time taking his son away when she'd agreed Luke could spend time with him? No. By God, no. She wouldn't do it to him again. If he had to steal a pair of J.D.'s handcuffs and shackle himself to her side, she wasn't walking out of his life again. Not like this. Not so soon.

Dazed, furious with pain and denial, he whipped into the parking spot next to hers. Fresh betrayal tasted bitter on his tongue. He slung open the car door and climbed out. "Where the hell do you think you're going?"

She blinked at him and plopped her hands on her hips. "Not that it's any of your business, and not that I for one minute like the tone of your voice, but I'm moving our things to Daddy's."

"You're not... Your dad's?"

She eyed him warily. "That's right. We're staying at his house."

Luke's knees went weak. His heart slid back into place and resumed a rocky beat. "Oh."

Beth's eyes widened. "You thought... Good grief, you thought I was leaving town and not telling you?"

Her accusatory tone didn't sit well. "It wouldn't be the first time."

"I've explained that. If you expect me to wallow in guilt for something that wasn't my fault, guess again, Luke. How's Daddy?"

Luke sighed and let her get away with changing the subject. "He was sleeping when I left."

"He's getting better, isn't he? He looks a lot better than he did when we got here."

"I won't deny he's improved, but I'll reserve judgment until I see what effect your mother has on him."

Her brow creased. "Good point."

"What happened when you left the hospital? Did you catch up with her? Where is she?"

"I caught up with her at Grandma's." Beth shook her head. "They were still yelling at each other when I left. Or rather, Mother was yelling. It's virtually impossible to have an argument with Grandma, because she won't argue. She did what was best for everyone, and that's all there is to it." She shook her head again. "She's not one bit sorry for all the lies she told, for all the lives she changed. There's not a single ounce of remorse in her body."

"What are you going to do? Have you decided how long you're staying?"

"I don't know." She turned toward the motel room, where she'd left the door open. "Right now I'm going to move our things to Daddy's, then get something to eat."

"Where's Ryan?"

She gave him a half smile over her shoulder. "He's learning the finer points of herding sheep from your dad."

Luke grinned slowly. "No kidding?"

"No kidding. He couldn't wait to get back out to the ranch today when Zach called and invited him. He's spending the night."

"How does that make you feel, him spending time with the Ryans?"

"I'm glad, Luke, When we left home, I didn't expect to find you here. Grandma told me years ago that you'd moved away. Then, when I saw you, when Ryan saw you and knew who you were, I was afraid he would resent you because of what I thought you'd done. Now that he knows you didn't deliberately turn your back on us, on me, well, that's a different story. He hasn't said it in so many words, but I can tell he's eager to get to know you and your family. He's never had a man in his life, Luke. He needs you."

Her words soothed the raw edges of Luke's nerves. "He's got me, Beth, you know that. But what happens when you decide to leave?" He held up his hand to keep her from answering. "Let me buy you dinner and we'll talk about it."

Beth took a deliberate step away "Not tonight, thanks. I want to get settled at Daddy's. If you have time, you could go out to the ranch. Ryan would like that."

Luke took a deep breath. He didn't much care for the way she backed away from him, nor for the look of wariness in her eyes. Then he thought, hell, maybe she was right. Maybe they were better off keeping a little distance between them. It wasn't as if they could just pick up where they'd left off sixteen years ago. They were different now. Different people with different lives, different priorities.

And his biggest priority right now was his son.

Beth pulled up at the curb before the tiny two-bedroom house on Stanolind and parked. She sat still a long moment and just looked. The neighborhood had aged some. The elms and cottonwoods planted back in the forties, when Stanolind Oil built these houses, had grown. A few looked as if they'd been replaced by younger trees. The house on the corner was blue, the one next to it green. They used to be white. Other than that, things looked pretty much the same. Mr. Bower still hadn't fenced his backyard. Two doors down from him, at Carol's old house, they still had that same huge evergreen. She wondered if Carol's folks still lived there. If they still put lights on that tree at Christmas.

At the house Beth had grown up in, nothing seemed to have changed. Same asbestos shingles painted white, same dark green trim. The house was still small, the sidewalk was still cracked, and marigolds still bloomed on either side of the front porch. The grass was as vibrantly green as it had always been this time of year. And it still had dandelions.

A flood of memories washed through her mind. Chasing a butterfly across the yard while her parents laughed and encouraged her from the front porch. Falling down and skinning her knees on the sidewalk. Raking fall leaves from beneath the cottonwood in back and the two elms in front into big piles, then leaping into the piles and scattering the leaves all over again. Following behind her daddy while he shoveled two feet of snow off the walk, then, when she was older, grumbling at having to do the shoveling herself.

The memories rolled across her vision, blurring it, lodging in her throat in a huge, hard lump. God, how she had missed this place. Maybe if she'd had the chance to say goodbye, the chance to decide for herself when it was time to leave, looking at it, remembering, wouldn't hurt so much.

But she'd had no such chances. She'd left on vacation, fully believing she'd be home in a mere two weeks.

"Damn you, Grandma. Damn you for stealing my life, my home, my love, my son's father. Damn you."

Beth allowed herself another full minute of grief and self-pity—and deep down, self-blame—before forcing the emotions away. She got out of the car and strode up the walk.

Next door, Mr. Bower came out on his porch. "Well, hello, Bethany," he called.

"Hi, Mr. Bower."

"Back from vacation, I see. Did you have a good time?"

The impulse to laugh shamed her. She'd already laughed at his poor memory once this week. It really wasn't funny that the old guy couldn't remember things. Still, it was hard to keep a straight face when she called back, "Yeah, but it's good to be back."

The key was under the doormat, just as her father had said it would be. Some things, it seemed, had changed. She never remembered their doors being locked, not once. Of course, with the key in such an obvious place, she didn't know what good her father hoped to accomplish by using the lock. With a shake of her head, she let herself inside the house.

More memories, more pain. Everything looked the same, from the nubby nylon wears-like-iron beige sofa to the Chinese lamp with its red silk shade trimmed in black silk fringe. Her daddy's big, sloppy rocker in one corner, the old blond desk in the other.

The same venetian blinds. She wondered wryly if that was the same dust—judging by the thickness of the layer, it was a definite possibility.

Through the doorway into the kitchen she could see the end of the chrome-legged table and one matching chair. The old gas stove where her mother had taught her to cook. The microwave and new refrigerator next to it startled her. With another glance around, she finally noticed a few other new items. The television next to the front door, a digital clock on the middle shelf of the bookcase beside the rocker.

Aside from those few items, the rest of the house looked as it had the day she and her mother had left. Stepping into her bedroom was like entering a time warp, falling down a tunnel and coming out sixteen years ago.

Her hand shook on the doorknob so hard the knob rattled. Her pom-poms. Sweet heavens, he'd left her pom-poms, one faded green, the other dingy white, hanging from the ceiling in the corner, exactly as she'd left them.

Oh, Daddy. How it must hurt him to see all the reminders day after day, year after year. Her dolls and stuffed animals—God, the green stuffed snake Luke had won her at the Rio Blanco County Fair during their junior year, still stretched out across her pink eyelet bedspread. Luke's senior picture still in its frame on her dresser, next to the comb, brush and mirror set Santa Claus had brought her when she was six.

Other relics leapt out at her one by one, sending her spiraling farther down the tunnel of years, from her earliest memories to her last days spent in this room. She staggered beneath their weight and slid to the floor, where she closed her eyes and took a deep, swift breath, praying for the tightness in her chest to ease.

From time to time over the years Luke had found himself in the uncomfortable position of being envious of his brother. Years ago, when it became obvious Beth wasn't coming home, when her grandmother's taunts about Beth marrying some doctor had finally sunk in, Luke hadn't been able to bear being around J.D.

At the time, Luke thought J.D. had it all—a wife, two beautiful children. The things Luke and Beth had planned for and talked about all during high school. Things he'd wanted so badly they'd left an acid taste in his mouth when he'd realized he would never have them. Not with Beth.

When J.D.'s wife walked out and left him to raise their two kids, Luke had still been envious. At least J.D. had his kids. Then last year, along had come Kat, and poor ol' J.D. had fallen for her so fast and so hard, Luke even envied J.D. his pain and confusion.

With his gaze drifting to Ryan washing up at the sink, Luke figured he didn't need to envy J.D. his kids anymore. Luke had a son of his own now—no matter that he'd missed the first fifteen years of the boy's life.

But the old envy was still there. Not bitter envy— it had never been bitter. Luke had never wished to take away what J.D. had, only wished that he, too, could have the same. Never had his envy been more sharp than now, as he watched J.D. reach out and stroke his wife's round abdomen to soothe the restless child growing in her womb.

He had missed that. Luke had been denied the right to watch Beth grow and ripen with his baby. He'd been denied a thousand things, all the things he'd said to Beth the other night in the car.

The way he figured, he could sit around and moan about all he'd missed, and let what little time he might have with his son slip away while he yearned to relive the last sixteen years, or he could pull himself together and go from here.

Watching his son kid around with J.D.'s son, Luke had no trouble making his choice.

"So, how'd it go today?" he asked Ryan when the boys came to the table.

Ryan gave him a sheepish grin. "You mean after I learned how to stay out of everybody's way?"

"No," his cousin Mike said with feigned sobriety, "he means after you learned which end of the horse was front and which was back."

"Here, now," Zach said. "Don't be pickin' on the boy. He did just fine."

"Yeah, since it was his first time and all," Sandy offered.

"Never mind first times." Zach slathered butter onto a slice of bread. "He did just fine."

"That's all right, Grandpa." Ryan didn't look the least affronted. "Mike's lying, anyway. I never had any trouble figuring out which end was which on the horse. Everybody knows that. It's just like a boat— the pointy end is on the front."

Luke let the laughter float around him and tried not to stare at his son, but it was hard. He never wanted to take his eyes off the boy who looked so much like him, the young man he and Beth had created together in love and lust in the front seat of his daddy's pickup.

When supper was over and the men had finished cleaning the kitchen—Kat had cooked, but put her foot down at another single lick of domesticity—Luke knew he wanted some time alone with Ryan. "How about a walk? If you want to be able to move tomorrow, you need to stretch the kinks out of those muscles."

"Okay."

They strolled across the backyard together. Luke headed them toward the creek at the base of the bluff about a quarter of a mile from the house.

"Did you see my mom today?"

"Yeah." Luke stuffed his hands into the hip pockets of his jeans. "At the hospital. Your grandmother's in town."

"Gran? No kidding?"

"Yeah. And I'm supposed to tell you that you and your mother are staying at your granddad's house now instead of the motel."

Ryan frowned and studied the ground carefully as he kept stride with Luke. After a few silent moments he asked, "Is Granddad gonna get well?"

"This time last week I wasn't so sure. But now, yeah, I really think he's going to be fine." After another silence, Luke asked, "So how'd it really go today?"

Ryan tried to hide his grin, then gave in and let it come. "It was great. But I think Grandpa had me doing stuff it would have been hard to screw up."

"You seem to be taking all this pretty well," Luke said cautiously.

"What do you mean?"

Luke shrugged. "Everything. All of us—this whole new family being thrown at you. Grandfathers, cousins, an aunt and uncle. Me. Knowing what you thought of me all your life, I guess I'm surprised you've been able to stop hating me so easily."

Ryan gave a shrug and watched a jackrabbit leap away from a clump of sagebrush and hightail it toward the hills.

"You did, didn't you?" Luke asked, his breath and heart on hold.

"Did what?"

"Stop hating me?"

Ryan's head whipped around toward Luke. "I don't hate you," he said in a rush. Then he ducked his head between his shoulders and looked away. "I...don't think I ever did, really."

Luke's heart started up again, and his breathing returned to normal. He rubbed a hand across his mouth, across his busted lip. "Could have fooled me. Not that I blame you, considering what you and your mother thought."

"Oh, that. Well, yeah, I guess...I don't know, it was just all mixed up. Mom never wanted me to hate you. I mean, she never told me you didn't want me or anything. She just said you didn't know about me, and that by the time *she* knew about me, it was too late."

Ryan could have no idea how his words affected Luke. Shock was the word that came closest to what he felt. Beth had thought he'd jilted her, had cheated on her with her best friend. Yet she hadn't wanted her son to hate him?

"It was different with Gran. She never had anything good to say about Granddad."

"Nor about me, I imagine."

Ryan shook his head. "She never said anything bad about you, except once when I was little. I don't even remember what she said, but I remember Mom yelling at her. Gran never said anything bad about you after that."

Luke stopped and squeezed his eyes shut. *Oh, God, Beth, thank you. Thank you for not making him hate me.*

"That thing at the hospital that first day, when I, uh, well, you know. That was...I guess that was...I don't know what it was. It was because I thought you'd hurt my mother. And I guess part of it was because I figured once you knew about me, you wouldn't want anything to do with me."

The fear and uncertainty in Ryan's voice nearly did Luke in. The guts it must have taken the kid to admit that. "You know better now, don't you?" Luke met his gaze and held it. "I want everything to do with you. Everything. I just don't want to...overwhelm you. I don't want you to think I'd try to step in and take over your life or anything like that. I guess I need to know what you want. I want to be your father, even though I don't think I know how. But I don't want to crowd you. For all I know, you don't want or need a dad. Maybe you'd just as soon I back off."

"No." The cry came, swift and desperate. Ryan blushed and looked away.

As if suffering the same need for movement, they

resumed walking toward the creek at the same instant. "No?" Luke asked, his heart pounding like runaway hoofbeats.

It took Ryan several moments of swallowing and blinking before he spoke again. "It's weird, you know? I mean, I guess you were right, I did hate you. I wanted a father and I figured it was your fault I didn't have one. But at the same time, I had this thing—I guess you'd call it a fantasy. One day you'd find out about me, and you'd come for us, for Mom and me, and you'd want us, and you'd be a real dad and everything, and we'd all be happy. Then we came here and found out there'd been a mistake, that you never got married, and suddenly I had a dad, and you didn't act mad about it or anything, about me, I mean. It was almost like all my wishes had come true."

The ground stopped abruptly before them. Luke concentrated on planting his feet, on not stepping off the three-foot drop into the creek. He couldn't have spoken just then if God Himself had commanded it. A magpie scolded them for intruding, then flew off, unlocking Luke's throat enough for speech.

He faced his son, watched him carefully avoid his gaze. "You're a pretty special kid, Ryan Martin. I'm proud you're my son."

Ryan swallowed hard and stared at the creek, his eyes wide to keep the tears from spilling. "Does that mean...you wouldn't mind... I mean, would it be all right if..." He stopped and swallowed again. "If I called you...Dad?"

Luke's knees nearly went out from under him. He

hadn't realized his own eyes were full until he felt them overflow. When he spoke, his voice cracked. "I'd be honored."

Chapter Eight

The next morning Beth visited her father and assured him she was now ensconced in his house. As the night had progressed, the memories in the house had grown less painful, softer, friendly, and she had felt more at ease in her old room than she'd at first feared. Leon was pleased she was once again under his roof, and said so.

After leaving him, she paid a visit to her grandmother's. It didn't take her more than a moment to realize two things. First, her mother and grandmother were barely speaking. That wasn't particularly surprising, under the circumstances. But something else was going on. There was something about the entire situation that they weren't telling her.

The flash of guilt in Margaret's eyes astounded Beth. What did her mother have to feel guilty about?

Unless... Oh, God, no. It was too cruel to even consider, yet with a tightening in her stomach, Beth
forced herself to consider it. The question poured out
before she could stop it. "Mother, did you know Luke
never married?"

Margaret's eyes flew wide. "No," she cried.
"Beth, no, I swear I would never have lied about
that."

Truth was there, in her eyes, in her voice. Beth
couldn't deny it. Yet there was something else, too.
Guilt. "Then what aren't you telling me?"

Margaret closed her eyes, took a deep breath, then
looked at Beth. "Nothing. There's nothing more to
tell."

Rose smirked. If that glimpse of something in Margaret's eyes hadn't alerted Beth, Rose's smirk certainly would have. There was definitely more that
wasn't being said. But pry as she might, Beth got no
answers from either woman. Frustrated, she left them
to their hostile silence and went home.

As she walked in the door of the house, the phone
was ringing.

"Hey, Mom."

Pleasure filled her at the sound of Ryan's voice.
She missed him. "Hi. How's everything going? Are
you having a good time?"

"Yeah, great. Listen, Mom, you haven't eaten supper yet, have you?"

"Since it's only three o'clock, no, I haven't."

"Good. Don't eat. We're bringing you a surprise."

"Who's we? What kind of surprise?"

"Dad and me. And it's an edible surprise." He
mumbled something to someone there with him, then

said into the phone, "We'll be there in about an hour." He hung up quickly, sounding eager and excited as he said goodbye.

Beth put the phone back in the cradle with hands that shook. Dad. He'd called Luke Dad. She wondered if Luke's throat ached with tears at the sound of it, the way hers did.

Dad, she thought again.

Then she cried. Damn, but she'd been doing a lot of that lately. But she couldn't help it. Her son was fifteen years old, and was just now able to call a man Dad.

"Grandma, why? Why did you do this to us? And God help me, why did I let you?"

Ryan and Luke showed up as promised an hour later, sunburned and wind tossed and grinning like two little boys digging their bare toes in forbidden mud. Beth took one look at them and fought to keep from grinning back. "What have you done?"

Ryan held a grocery bag in one arm and pulled open the storm door with the other. Luke carried an ice chest straight past her and into the kitchen and put it on the counter next to the sink. Ryan followed, set the brown bag on the kitchen table, then stood beside Luke and faced her.

Luke rested his forearm on Ryan's shoulder. "Keep in mind, I'm not criticizing the way you've raised him—I think you've done a terrific job. But, Beth, you have sorely neglected one very important aspect of this young man's education."

Beth crossed her arms and pursed her lips. They would never begin to understand how much it thrilled her to see the two of them standing side by side, looking so much alike, looking so happy together. Looking like a pair of smug co-conspirators. She felt thrilled, and hurt, and guilty, because this shouldn't be the first time.

She shook her head. The negative emotions had no place in this house that felt as if it was about to burst forth with joyous laughter any moment. She might never forgive her grandmother or herself, but she had to let go of the past before the pain and guilt interfered with the budding relationship between Ryan and his father. She would not allow anything to stop them from getting to know each other.

"Okay," she said, "I'll bite. What part of his education have I neglected?"

Ryan poked an elbow into Luke's ribs. "She'll bite." Ryan started laughing. "That's a good one. She'll bite." He laughed so hard he staggered, and Luke was right there laughing and staggering with him.

"Would one of you care to tell me what's so funny?"

Luke's laughter ended on a heavy sigh as he looked down at Ryan. "She used to have a sense of humor, you know, back when I knew her."

"She still does," Ryan said, still grinning. "But I don't think she gets the joke. Guess we'll have to show her about my newly expanded education."

"Allow me." Luke reached over and opened the lid of the ice chest just enough to reach his hand inside. The smell of fish rolled across the room. Ice cubes rattled. Then, with a flourish, Luke pulled out his prize. "How could a good Colorado girl like you raise a son to the advanced age of fifteen without teaching him about trout?''

Beth felt her grin slip loose. In his hand Luke held a beautiful, colorful rainbow trout. ''I plead guilty, but only because the only rainbow trout you find in Kansas City are the ones shipped in to fancy restaurants. And believe me, ordering them from a menu just isn't the same as catching them yourself.'' As her stomach rumbled in anticipation of one of her absolutely favorite foods, her grin widened. ''How many did you get?''

Luke beamed. ''Five. Ryan got two of them himself.''

''Yeah, wow, Mom, you shoulda seen how they fought.''

The two regaled her with tales of the morning's adventures as Beth unloaded the grocery bag. A loaf of French bread, three large baking potatoes, a can of corn, a head of lettuce, two ripe tomatoes, a tub of margarine, a half pound of Longhorn cheddar, a bottle of Italian salad dressing and two pints of fresh strawberries.

''I didn't know what Leon had in his cupboards, so we bought everything we could think of for the meal.''

''A good thing,'' she told him. ''I haven't even looked, much less gone shopping.'' She eyed the old gas range, then the trout Luke was rinsing off in the sink.

''What's that look mean?'' Luke asked.

She sighed. ''I'll probably burn them. I haven't used a gas stove in years.''

Luke hovered protectively over the sinkful of fish

and gave her a look of horror. "You can't burn our fish," he cried. "We braved the terrors of the wilderness, fought off wild animals and man-eating insects to catch these fish."

Ryan hooted with laughter.

Beth stuck her nose in the air. "Wild animals and man-eating insects. Ha. I doubt you had much trouble defending yourselves against jackrabbits and mosquitoes."

Ryan laughed harder. "She got you there, Dad."

Dad. There it was again. Beth felt her heart squeeze.

"Yeah, well," Luke said, still guarding the sink, "she can handle the rest of the meal, but I'll cook the fish."

"Sounds fine to me," Beth said.

"I'm gonna go bring in my clothes. Where do I put them?" Ryan asked.

"Find a place in my room."

"Which one is yours?"

"The one with the pink ruffles," Luke volunteered. Then, with eyes wide, he immediately clamped his mouth shut. He ducked his head and turned toward the sink, but not before Beth and Ryan both saw a blush stain his cheeks.

Beth felt an answering blush of her own.

Ryan blinked. He drew his hand down hard over his mouth and tugged the corners down with his thumb and forefinger in an unsuccessful attempt to keep from grinning. "Never mind," he said, pursing his lips. "I won't ask how you knew that. I'm outa here."

The only sound in the house after Ryan slammed

out the front door was the clink of ice cubes shifting as they melted in the open ice chest.

Still facing the sink, Luke heaved a sigh. "I'm sorry. I shouldn't have said that. It just...slipped out. I didn't mean to embarrass you."

Beth caught herself copying her son's earlier gesture of trying to tug the grin from her lips with her fingers. She finally gave up and laughed. "I think you embarrassed yourself."

He peered at her over his shoulder, and finally his tense expression relaxed. "Yeah. I think I did. At the clinic I talk to teenagers about sex all the time, but this...this is different. This was my son, our son, and I was alluding to us. Yes, I definitely embarrassed myself." He shook his head with chagrin and went back to rinsing the fish.

Beth waited until he turned off the water, then said softly, "He called you Dad."

At the sink, Luke went still. "Yeah. He, uh, yesterday he asked if he could."

"It must sound funny to you to hear a grown boy calling you that," she said carefully. "How do you feel about it?"

He finished drying his hands on a cup towel and turned slowly to face her. A dozen emotions crossed his eyes as he met her gaze. "I feel proud. Honored. Humble." One corner of his mouth quirked up. "Scared spitless. Intimidated as hell."

She matched his wry grin. "Welcome to the wonderful world of parenthood. I've known him all his life, and I still feel those exact same things when I look at him and realize he came from me. Live with him on a day-to-day basis and you can add wonder, frustration, amazement. Love.''

His eyes darkened. ''Will I ever get to do that, Beth?''

''Do what?''

''I already love him, but will I ever get to live with him on a day-to-day basis?''

Sudden, shocking terror streaked through her. Ryan live with Luke? ''What are you asking? You can't mean you want to take him away—''

''No!'' Luke sprang forward and gripped her shoulders. ''No, Beth, no. I'd never try to take him away from you. That's not what I meant. Hell, I don't know what I meant. I just want to be part of his life.''

Beth read the sincerity in his eyes. Aside from that, she knew Luke so well, or had, at one time. He was fair and honest and would never hurt anyone, certainly not his own son. Hopefully not his son's mother. The tension eased out of her. ''We'll work something out, somehow.''

''I know we will.'' He let go of her shoulders and stepped back. ''Together.''

''Together,'' she agreed.

The sudden heat that flared in his eyes startled her. She felt an answering heat deep inside her own body. Lord, how long had it been since she'd felt such stirrings spiral through her?

Years, came the answer. With the exception of the night he'd kissed her at her motel room door, it had been years. Sixteen of them.

Rattled by the feelings rushing through her, the heat simmering in her blood, she reached blindly for the head of lettuce on the table behind her. "Come on," she said with forced lightness. "Let's cook."

His eyes darkened. He ran his gaze slowly down her body, then back up again, making her feel as though he had stroked her with his hands. With barely a hint of a smile, he said, "Any time you say, babe."

Out on the front porch Ryan paused with one hand on the handle of the storm door, the other gripping his duffel bag. He couldn't make out the words his dad said, but the look in his eyes was unmistakable. Good gravy, his dad was hot for his mother!

Yes! he hollered in his mind. Yes, yes. A thousand times yes.

Carefully, silently, he backed off the porch and out of sight of the door and prayed with all his might. He hadn't told his dad everything yesterday about his daydreams, his fantasies. Ryan had barely mentioned the part where his mom and dad would get back together and the three of them would live together and be a real family.

'Course, not that Ryan had ever seen a real family, a happy one, in real life. Jon Murphy's dad got drunk on weekends and beat up on the rest of the family— and they all lied about it to everybody. To hear them tell it, Jon, his mom and his younger brother were always falling off the porch or running into a door. Carla Harrison's mom was sleeping with the guy down at the dry cleaners. Bonnie Harter's dad made passes at anything in skirts, while Bonnie's mom cried a lot.

Most of the rest of the kids he knew lived with one

parent and saw the other one once in a while on weekends or something, if at all.

Still, Ryan knew what he wanted his own family to be like. He wanted them all to care about and respect each other, to do things together and have fun together.

He stood at the edge of the flower bed beside the porch and pictured playing ball, with both his parents cheering from the stands. Going somewhere, the three of them, on vacation like other families did. Camping, maybe, in someplace like Yellowstone or the Redwoods. His dad teaching him to drive while Mom nagged at them to be careful. His parents kissing each other in front of the Christmas tree.

On and on the family pictures rolled through his hungry heart. When he heard the clank of a skillet on the stove and the rush of water from the kitchen faucet, he figured they'd gone back to fixing supper.

"Hang cool, man," he whispered to himself. His parents weren't likely to get back together in one night, no matter how badly Ryan wanted them to. But he would watch and do what he could to help things along, and, please God, it would happen soon. Before his mom decided it was time to go home.

Whistling a tune he made up as he went, Ryan made as much noise as possible going in the front door and heading for his mother's room. The one with the pink ruffles. It was all he could do to keep from laughing with excitement. So his dad remembered what his mother's bedroom looked like, after all these years.

Ain't life grand?

* * *

Ryan got in the way for a while in the kitchen, then backed off and left his parents alone, trying not to be too obvious as he watched them. Oh, yeah, there was definitely something in the air around here besides the smell of fish. Sparks were flying.

When their arms accidentally brushed, his dad's eyes got all dark and his nostrils flared, while Mom jerked away like she'd been zapped by a bolt of lightning. The next time, even Ryan, with his limited experience in such things, could tell there was nothing accidental in the way his dad's hand slid across his mother's stomach.

The way she sucked in her breath as her gaze flew to Luke's had Ryan glancing sharply away. It seemed too personal a thing for him to watch. But he was glad it was happening. He'd never been so damn glad about anything in his whole life.

Except maybe catching his first trout.

Ryan told his trout stories again the next day to Leon. Beth chuckled as the size of those fish grew with the telling.

"When I get out of here," Leon said, "you'll have to take me to that exact same spot so I can try my hand. I'm a pretty fair fisherman myself."

"When you get out of here," Luke said, strolling into the room and startling Beth, "you're going to go home and take it easy."

He was a good doctor, Beth thought, and a good friend to her father to come in in the middle of his week off and check on him. And she knew her father wasn't the only patient Luke visited. She'd seen him down the hall when she and Ryan had come in. She was so proud—of Luke, for Luke, for what he'd made of his life. Proud of the man he'd become.

"Will he get to go home soon?" she asked.

Luke answered her, but kept his gaze on Leon. "If he behaves himself and continues improving, I think we might spring him Sunday."

"Ah, hell," Leon muttered. "Why not now?"

"You want a relapse?"

Luke won the ensuing argument, but he had a sneaky feeling Beth was the one who convinced Leon to stay put. Luke had to wonder if he was keeping Leon in the hospital for Leon's own good, or because deep down Luke feared that as soon as Leon was discharged, Beth would go home.

The thought of her leaving almost undid him. Hot panic nearly suffocated him. He didn't want her to leave town. But then he had to ask himself another question. Did he want her to stay so he could be with his son, or was he letting the kiss he and Beth had shared outside her motel room influence him?

Both. There was no question that he didn't want her to take Ryan away. But the other... He didn't know why he should be surprised that all the old fire was still there between them. He'd never gotten her out of his blood.

What he wasn't sure of was, was what he was feeling real? Honest desire for who she now was? Or was it merely a nostalgic yearning to relive his youth? Was he attracted to the girl or the woman?

The girl had always been his dream, beautiful and loving. The woman, from what he could tell, had lived up to the promise. One thing was for certain—

he wasn't ready for her to walk out of his life again. Not yet. Maybe not ever.

And that worried him.

As she watched Ryan and Luke leave the hospital together on their way to do "man things," like wash and wax Luke's Mark VII, Beth's thoughts ran parallel to Luke's. Was it the man who attracted her, or the memory of what they'd once shared?

If only he hadn't called her *babe* again yesterday. Luke was the only person who had ever called her that, and she still went weak in the knees at the way his voice dropped low and turned husky when he said it. Over the years she had convinced herself that she had never melted at the sound of a man's voice. It had been her imagination, teenage hormones, or something.

But her hormones weren't teenaged any longer, and neither was she. She was a grown woman with a nearly grown son and a job she had to return to in the very near future. She had called her office to let them know how to reach her, and had told them she'd be back next week.

Yet at the thought of leaving Rangely, leaving Luke, leaving her dad, her mind and heart screamed in protest. There was something…unfinished between her and Luke. They'd never had the chance to say goodbye, and, given the opportunity back then, she knew they never would have parted.

So what now? Was she supposed to be able to simply go back to Kansas City and resume her life? What about Ryan?

"Are you gonna leave when I get home?"

Her father's voice startled her. She jerked toward him, not knowing what to say. She ended up shrugging and looking away.

Luke had been right about one thing—the Martin cupboards were bare. With her father due home tomorrow, Beth needed to do something about the situation. That afternoon she drove down Main Street to Bestway and parked. God, more memories. But these were fun ones. Sneaking down Main—some sneaking; it had always been in broad daylight—and crossing the street when she knew full well she was forbidden to cross Main, just so she could slip into Bestway for a candy bar.

Of course, she could have gotten a candy bar at several other places without having to cross Main and break that specific rule, but other stores wanted cash money. Bestway, bless them, would let her sign her parents' card and charge her purchases.

As she stepped into the familiar old store, she laughed silently at the illogic of the youthful mind. Her parents had always known, every single time, what she'd done. Idiot that she'd been, it had taken her nearly two years to figure out that all they had to do was look at their charge card and spot her scrawling signature.

With a shake of her head, Beth got a grocery cart and started down the narrow aisles. Maybe, just for old times' sake, she would sign her father's card and charge the groceries to him.

Her mind was only half on her shopping, the other half wondering if she would run into anyone she knew. In front of the dairy case, with the musty smell of refrigerated air threatening to make her sneeze, she did. At Beth's breathless gasp, Carol Thompson—no, Carol Howard now—looked up. Their gazes collided, locked. Beth had hated Carol for so many years, it was hard, in that split instant of connection, to remember it had all been based on a lie.

She looked the same. Her skin was still pale and smooth, and her short red hair still curled around her narrow face. Her eyes were still as wide, still as green as ever.

The years rolled away and the two women looked at each other through years of childhood secrets and adolescent dreams. First roller skates and kittens. The first time their parents had taken them ice skating when Douglas Creek froze over. First bras, first pimples, first hair spray, first dance, first dates.

Beth saw the instant when Carol remembered that her best friend had disappeared without a word years ago, never contacting her once. The betrayal, then ice, sprang sharply into Carol's eyes.

"Well, well, well. I wondered if you'd ever have the nerve to show your face in this town again." The disdain in her voice cut Beth to the quick.

"Hello, Carol."

"Does Luke know you're here? Your little disappearing act damn near killed him, you know."

"Carol, I can explain."

"I don't want your explanation. You couldn't be bothered with me all these years, I can't be bothered with you now. Excuse me. I'm busy." Carol maneuvered her shopping cart in the narrow aisle until she had it aimed in the opposite direction.

"Carol, wait," Beth cried. She didn't blame Carol

for the way she felt. Had she not learned the truth herself, she might have acted even worse. But she couldn't let the lie live, wouldn't take the blame solely on her shoulders for what had happened. "Carol, I didn't come back, I never contacted you or anyone else because my grandmother told me you and Luke got married just when I was due back from vacation."

The items in Carol's cart tumbled over themselves when she jerked to a halt at the end of the aisle. She turned slowly, shock widening her eyes. "She told you *what?*"

Beth swallowed and gripped the handle of her cart. "That you and Luke got married. That you had to."

"And you *believed* her?" Carol shrieked.

Beth squeezed her eyes shut. She'd never get through this if she had to look Carol in the eyes. "Out of the blue, my parents were splitting, and Mother told me Daddy didn't want anything more to do with us. I was scared and confused and my whole world seemed like it was coming apart…and then I found out I was pregnant. I was frantic to get home. Then Grandma said that about you and Luke."

Beth opened her eyes and made herself meet Carol's wounded, outraged gaze. "I think if the unthinkable hadn't been happening—if Mother and Daddy hadn't been splitting up right then—I might have come home anyway. But it was just all too much at once, and I couldn't handle it, didn't know what to do. So, yes," she added softly, "ashamed as I am to admit it, I believed what Grandma told me. I had no reason to think that of you and Luke, but I had no reason to imagine my own grandmother would make something like that up, either. I was young and stupid and gullible. I was hurt, and way too proud to call and see if it was true. In the state I was in, I couldn't bear to be laughed at if it was. Pretty poor excuses, but that's how it happened.''

Carol put a hand to her mouth. ''My God. You mean you've spent all these years thinking...thinking Luke and I betrayed you?''

In the next aisle Luke stood frozen, one hand on a six-pack of soft drinks, the voices from over at the dairy case floating over the cardboard display on top of the shelf between him and the next aisle. His breath came fast. He tried to quiet it, not wanting to miss what Beth was saying, and felt guilty for eavesdropping. But he couldn't stop.

Beth had told him the same thing, only this time he heard more. He heard the devastating pain she had gone through. It soaked into his bones and nearly crippled him there on the linoleum.

At least he'd still had his family, his home, his friends. Beth had been left with nothing but her mother. No hopes, no friends, no home, shut away from everything familiar. Just the clothes in her suitcase, a baby on the way and a whole life lost.

The words from the next aisle grew faint as the buzzing in his ears drowned them out. Carefully, quietly, so he wouldn't give away his presence, he backed down the aisle and fled the store.

Beth and Carol met each other halfway between the butter and the skim milk, arms hugging, emotions overwhelming and tears washing away sixteen years of bitterness and hurt feelings.

"I've missed you—"

"I can't believe—"

They spoke at once, then stopped. They backed away a little, but each kept one hand on the other, afraid to sever the connection. Both wiped at their tears. Matching sheepish grins wobbled on their lips.

"Look at us," Carol said.

"Yeah." Beth sniffed and tried to laugh, but it came out more as a choked sob. "Pretty pathetic, huh, right here in the grocery store?"

Carol let out a watery chuckle. Then with a short gasp, she checked her watch. "Oh, damn, I'm gonna be late, and they're all waiting for me." She gripped Beth's hands. "What are you doing tonight?"

"Well—"

"Cancel it. You have to come over. It's Jerry's birthday, and we always throw a big party. Say you'll..." Her voice cut off and her eyes widened. "Pregnant? Did you say you were pregnant?"

"I have the most gorgeous fifteen-year-old son in the world."

"No kidding?" Carol let out a whoop. "Fifteen? Same age as my oldest daughter. Fifteen, huh? That means..."

"Yes, it does. And even if I tried to deny it, one look would tell the truth. He's the spitting image of Luke."

"Oh, my God, does Luke know?"

"He does now. It came as quite a shock at first, but Ryan and Luke are getting to know each other."

Carol's grin was outrageous. "You named him

Ryan? Gad, girl, you've got guts. Come tonight, bring him. Everybody'll be there. Please, you have to.''

"I'd love to. Where do you live?"

"Same place I've lived all my life. Mom and Pop moved to Grand Junction years ago and bought a condo. Jerry and I bought the old house from them."

Beth shook her head. "I'm staying at Daddy's. I can't believe we haven't run into each other before this."

"We've been on vacation. Just got back yesterday, and tonight's our annual bash. Come any time. The party officially starts at seven."

"Can I bring anything?"

"Just that son of yours. I can't wait to meet him."

Chapter Nine

Jerry Howard's thirty-fifth birthday party—complete
with crepe paper streamers, a giant "Happy Birthday,
Old Man" sign, and dozens of gag gifts—was loud,
crowded and boisterous, and Beth couldn't remember
the last time she'd had so much fun. She saw old
friends and met new ones, ate hors d'oeuvres until
she felt full as a tick on a hound and, living danger-
ously, grabbed her second bottle of beer just before
ten o'clock.

There were at least forty adults crowded into the
tiny house, spilling down into the basement and out
into the yard, with nearly the same number of teenagers. Little ones had been left with baby-sitters for
the night. In the backyard under the glare of flood-
lights, a hot volleyball match was under way, teen-

aged boys against their dads—a tradition, Carol said, that had started about four years ago.

"Luke's sure not making any bones about who that boy belongs to, is he?" Carol said as Beth watched Ryan spike the ball over the net.

"No." As usual when she saw her son and his father together these days, Beth's eyes misted. "No bones at all."

"And?"

Beth tore her gaze from the slice of bare belly revealed as Luke raised his arms and jumped to return the ball. Her breath was faster than it should have been, as was her pulse. Looking away was harder than it should have been, too, but she managed to face Carol with what she hoped was a calm expression. "And what?"

Carol rolled her eyes. "Come on. You may have been gone all these years, but this is still me, girl. How do you feel about Luke publicly claiming your son like that?"

"He's Luke's son, too."

"Well." Carol raised a brow and grinned. "Guess that answers that, huh? Come on. I need another beer."

With their arms slung around each other's shoulders, the two women headed back into the throng of wall-to-wall people inside the house. The roar of dozens of voices was as loud as the backwash of a jet engine. Yet even with all the commotion, Beth was sure she could feel the floor throbbing beneath her feet with the beat of the rock music blasting down in the basement where the rest of the kids, and several adults, were dancing.

Looking around Carol's living room, Beth thought it was uncanny how little change she saw in so many of the faces around her. People she hadn't seen since high school were instantly recognizable. Well, most of them, anyway. Then there was Nancy Price, who'd been a beanpole in school and now looked like a sumo wrestler. And Lord have mercy, she was married to Paul Sanchez—and just look at him! In school, Paul had been overweight and pimply, with crooked teeth and bad breath. Now he was nothing short of magnificent! Broad shoulders, narrow hips, smooth, dark skin, and the whitest, straightest teeth in the room.

"Hard to believe, isn't it?" Carol whispered, noticing Beth gaping at Paul. "The kicker is, he's now the town dentist. Who'd have thought he'd turn out to be such a hunk?"

"Not me, I'm ashamed to say."

"And I'll tell you this. Despite how she's let herself go, Paul absolutely worships the ground Nancy waddles on."

"Carol! How catty. Shame."

"Well, I can't help it. I just get so damn mad. Look at her over there shoveling in the food. She eats constantly, and the things she eats, good grief."

"If she's happy, what do you care how she looks?"

"But that's my point," Carol said. "She's not happy, she's miserable, which is why she eats so much. She was doing really well there for a while. Looked good and took good care of herself. Then J.D. had to bust their oldest boy, Wade, on drug charges, and off she went to the nearest feed trough. I don't think she's stopped eating for long enough to do anything but sleep in the six months since."

Beth shivered and rubbed her arms. *There, but for the grace of God and a terrific son, go I.* She thanked her lucky stars that Ryan had never been involved with drugs, had never been in any serious trouble.

She spent the next hour visiting, joking, explaining with as few details as possible where she'd been since high school. Eventually she ended up downstairs listening to the music and watching the dancing.

Crepe paper streamers like the ones upstairs draped from the basement ceiling and hung down the walls. Colored lights from two opposite corners of the big room spun lazy shades of red and blue, green and gold, across the dancers.

Loud rock music poured from a boom box in the corner, with dozens of couples, young, middle-aged and older, bopping to the beat of the latest from Hootie and the Blowfish. Ryan had left the volleyball competition and was dancing with Diane, Carol and Jerry's oldest daughter. The two could have been mistaken for Carol and Luke at that age.

"Startling, isn't it, how much she looks like her mother?"

Beth turned toward Jerry's voice at her shoulder. "Yes."

"And your son, damn, Beth, he looks so much like Luke, seeing him makes me feel like I'm back in high school."

"I know what you mean." Beth grinned. "Diane's terrific, the way she's been introducing Ryan to all her friends."

Jerry heaved a heavy sigh. "I think she likes him."

Beth would have felt better if Jerry hadn't sounded so unhappy with the idea of his daughter liking her son. Her maternal instincts kicked in and brought a defensive angle to her jaw. "That bothers you?"

"Hell, she's my baby," Jerry cried. "She can't like boys."

Relieved and feeling a little abashed at her defensiveness, Beth chuckled. "Feeling our age, are we?"

"It's my birthday," Jerry said with irritation. "I'm supposed to feel my age. But actually, I should have expected this," he added with a nod toward their children. They appeared totally absorbed with one another and the fast beat of the music. "I should have known one look at him and she'd be a goner."

"Why is that?"

Jerry laughed. "She's had a crush on Luke since she was four years old."

"All right, you guys, break it up." Carol grabbed Jerry by the arm. "I want to dance with the birthday boy." She dragged her husband off to the dance floor and looped her arms around his neck. Oblivious to anyone who might be watching, Jerry spread both hands across her backside. Carol laughed and wiggled suggestively against him.

Beth sat to one side on the stairs, smiling, watching the dancing and sipping her third beer of the night. When the song ended, another began, this one slow, soulful, evocative. Linda Ronstadt's "Blue Bayou."

A hand brushed Beth's shoulder. She turned to find Luke lowering himself beside her. He raised his beer bottle, and Beth watched, mesmerized, as those lips that had always tempted her pressed themselves to the mouth of the bottle as if in slow motion. He took a long pull. His Adam's apple rose and fell twice, capturing her gaze, creating in her a hunger that startled her with its abrupt intensity. The bottle came away from his mouth slowly. When he licked his lips, she caught herself licking her own.

He was watching her. She couldn't see his eyes for staring at his mouth, but she knew he was watching her. When he spoke, his voice was deep and intimate. "It's been a long time since we danced."

Slowly she raised her gaze. His vivid blue eyes sent messages of heat and hunger that started a shiver down her spine and a like hunger deep inside her.

"Want to give it a try?" he asked.

She swallowed. "What?"

His eyes flashed a hotter message and the corners of his mouth curved up slightly. "Dancing. I asked if you wanted to dance."

Nerves fluttered in her stomach. Yes, she wanted to dance with him. She wanted to feel his arms around her, lay her head on his shoulder, feel his heart, the security of those arms that looked so strong. But what good would it do to stir up all the old feelings? And she had no doubt that would happen, just as it had when he'd kissed her.

Before she could come up with an answer, Luke took her by the hand and pulled her to her feet. "Come on. Be brave." He smiled a crooked smile and led her down the steps and in among the throng. "It's just a dance."

It should have been just a dance, but the instant he pulled her close, she knew it wasn't. Couples pressed near on all sides and swayed around them. Luke took her in his arms. Not the standard dance position where he put one hand on her waist, she put one on his shoulder, and their other hands clasped. No, not Luke, not with Beth. He locked his hands together at the base of her spine and pulled her lower body flush against his, the way they used to dance in high school. The contact was more intimate than the kiss they had shared in front of her motel room. Her heart raced, and somewhere deep inside, a melting warmth pulsed and spread through her arms and legs.

Their lips may not have touched this time, but the soulful music bound them together, flowing through them, tugging on old emotions, creating new ones. Every nerve in her body tingled to life. She didn't want this, didn't want to feel the things he made her feel, didn't want to want the things he made her want.

Luke spread his hands wide and slipped them up her back, slowly pressing until her breasts brushed his chest. Linda sang about going back someday. Luke pulled Beth closer until they were pressed flush against each other. Her heart pounded harder. Her blood rushed faster.

They didn't speak. He maneuvered her the way he wanted her, and she let him. He pulled her arms around his neck and pushed her head to his shoulder, then laid his cheek against the top of her head. She felt his chest expand on a deep breath.

His voice rumbled in her ear. "Feels good, doesn't it?"

"Yeah, it does."

"Like old times."

She raised her head and met his warm gaze. "Don't, Luke."

"Don't what?"

The colored lights on either side of the room were out of sync. While one cast a golden glow on one side of Luke's face, the other side was painted red, making him look like some sort of bronzed sun god. "There's no point in reliving old times. Daddy'll be out of the hospital tomorrow, then I'll be going home."

Luke's eyes darkened and his hold strengthened. "Why?"

"Why?" She swallowed, trying to moisten her dry mouth. "Because that's where I live. I have a house, a job to go back to."

A muscle in his jaw flexed. "And a man, maybe?"

"That's none of your business."

"What if I want it to be?"

She shook her head. "Don't, Luke."

He sighed and arched his neck as if to look at the ceiling, but his eyes were closed. "A house and a job. I notice you didn't say friends, or home." He looked down at her then, probing into her mind, searching out her secrets, her vulnerabilities. "You didn't say you had a life to go back to."

Beth stiffened under his too-accurate shot. "Don't put words in my mouth."

"I'm not. I'm pointing out the ones that weren't there."

"Well, for your information, of course I have friends."

"Like me?"

"What's that supposed to mean?"

"I used to be your friend, Beth. Your best friend. And you were mine."

There it was again, that tugging at old emotions,

old hopes, old heartaches. She steeled herself against them, against him. "That was a long time ago."

"Some things don't go away." The music swelled around them, through them, as if binding them together. Luke's thighs brushed hers, and his hands splayed across her lower back, massaging taut muscles through her shirt. "It's still there," he murmured. "I feel it. I know you feel it, too."

"Luke—"

"Don't go home yet, Beth. We've got a class reunion in a couple of weeks. Stay till then."

Stay? she thought frantically. Stay and let these feelings grow? She would have to be a class A fool, but then, it wouldn't be the first time. Nervously she said, "Whoever heard of a sixteen-year reunion?"

He shrugged. "We waited too late to plan one last year, so we're going in with the class behind us."

She shook her head again. "I can't just hang around for two more weeks. I've got a job to get back to."

"Will they give you leave?"

"Without pay, maybe. This trip is coming off my vacation time, and I'm almost out."

"I've got an idea."

She didn't trust his smile. Not for a minute. Not so much for what he meant by it, but for the way it made her heart pound.

"You're an office manager at a doctors' clinic, right?"

"Right." There was a trap here somewhere. She felt it ready to spring shut on her.

"Rangely Family Medicine happens to be short one office manager these days. If you can stay, you could fill in at the clinic until we hire someone permanent. That'll give you something to do with your days, and temporary income. Probably not as much money as you're used to in the big city, and certainly not what you're worth, but it would let you stay, give me more time with Ryan, you more with your dad."

"I don't—"

He put his fingers over her lips. "Just think about it, that's all I ask. Think about it."

He wasn't smiling now, but asking seriously, urging her with his eyes and voice to consider his idea. She shouldn't. Lord, no, she shouldn't. She and Luke couldn't simply pick up where they'd left off, and she didn't think she could bear to be around him and just be friends. The best thing for everyone would be for her and Ryan to go home. But when she opened her mouth she said, "All right, I'll think about it."

When the song ended and Luke didn't release her, Beth started to push away. Then the Righteous Brothers started singing "Unchained Melody," and as the lyrics spoke of hungering for a touch, Luke pulled her to his chest once more. With a sigh of surrender, maybe relief, she settled her head on his shoulder.

"Was that a beer I saw you drinking earlier?" he asked.

Beth frowned. "Why?"

With his nose and lips, he played with the spot behind her ear, sending hot shivers racing down her arms. "I was just wondering if alcohol still has the same effect on you as it used to."

"Class reunions and old jokes. Is the music making you feel nostalgic?"

He slid a hand up into her hair and pulled until she

raised her head and met his teasing gaze. "No, but you are. I was just curious if booze still turns you on."

Her lips quirked. "Shame on you. I can't believe you're teasing me about that."

"Not teasing." But he was smiling. "Just curious. Want me to get you another beer?"

She shouldn't have laughed, but she couldn't help it. "It wouldn't matter if you did."

"Why? Doesn't it affect you like that anymore?"

Maybe Beth was feeling nostalgic, too. Suddenly she didn't feel like laughing any longer, nor teasing. Her smile faded. "It was never the alcohol, Luke."

"Yeah? What was it then?"

"You. Only you."

"Oh, God." He dropped his head until his mouth rested against her shoulder. His arms tensed and squeezed tight. "I can't believe you said that. Not now, not here, when our son's only a few feet away and so many other people are all around and I can't..." With a hand to her lower back, he pressed her closer until she felt the suddenly hard ridge of flesh behind the fly of his jeans.

A corresponding softening took place down deep inside her. She moaned against his neck.

"Yeah," he said with a choked whisper. "My sentiments exactly. And for the record, no woman has ever been able to do this to me before with just words."

"I'm sorry. I shouldn't have said that."

"Yes," he hissed. "You should have. Say it again."

A shaky laugh escaped her lips. "Not on your life,

Dr. Ryan. Think of something disgusting to get your mind off the subject. Think about sheep dung or toads or something.''

Luke chuckled in her ear. ''Right now the only thing that comes to mind when I think of toads is horny toads.''

''That's horned toads, and you know it.''

His chest rose against hers on a deep breath. ''God, I've missed you, Beth.''

She squeezed her eyes shut on the sudden sting of tears. ''No more, Luke, please.''

''All right,'' he promised. His hand ran up and down her back, slowly, soothing her taut nerves, bringing other nerves to life. ''No more. For now.''

When the Righteous Brothers finished, Beth once again tried to pull away. ''You can't,'' Luke said, holding on tight. He gave her a wry grin. ''Not yet. I'm not...presentable.''

She gave him a questioning look. In answer, he nudged his hips against hers, letting her feel his hard arousal. With a swallow and a blush, she danced the next one with him while he thanked heaven the song was another slow one.

Diane and Ryan ended up dancing next to them, but the kids were so engrossed in each other, they didn't notice Beth and Luke.

Neither, apparently, did the tall, broad-shouldered young man who shoved another couple out of his way to reach Diane and Ryan. His voice carried over the quiet strains of ''In My Room'' by the Beach Boys. ''All right, Diane, enough's enough. You're supposed to be dancing with me.''

Diane gave a toss of vibrant red curls. "Says who? I'd rather dance with Ryan. See you later, Wade."

"Who's that?" Beth whispered to Luke.

"He's trouble. Wade Sanchez."

"Paul and Nancy's boy? The one J.D. busted?"

"Boy, you sure are up on things."

Wade Sanchez nudged Ryan's shoulder. "I heard about you. You're the one everybody's talkin' about. Doc Ryan's bastard."

The loud voice had couples stopping to stare. Against Beth, Luke stiffened. "Wait," she whispered to him. "Let Ryan handle it."

Ryan gave Diane an apologetic smile, then released her and turned to face the larger boy. "That's me," he said, offering his hand. "Ryan Martin."

Against Beth's ear Luke let out a soft whistle of admiration.

Wade sneered at Ryan's offer of a handshake. "I don't shake hands with bastards."

Beth held Luke back while Ryan heaved a resigned sigh. "Look. The word *bastard* doesn't offend me, because it's true, okay? But I have to admit I don't much care for your tone."

"Oh, yeah? What gutter was your mother hanging out in when your father found her?"

Luke flinched and moved to push Beth away. "No," she whispered. "He's a kid. You can't hit somebody else's kid."

"Wanna watch me?" Luke asked in a low growl.

But Beth held him back.

At the same time Ryan let out a low snarl. Before he could move, Diane stepped between him and Wade. "You can't hit him," Diane told Ryan.

"Oh, yeah," Ryan said, his glare centered on Wade. "Yeah, I can."

"No," Diane said emphatically. "If you hit him, he'll stumble into Jeff there, behind him. I know, 'cause Wade's always been clumsy. And Jeff's never liked Wade, so Jeff'll shove him back. Then Tony will hit Jeff, because Tony's Wade's friend, and Wade will hit you back, and before you know it, the whole room will be fighting, and there's at least two city cops and one county deputy upstairs, and they'd probably end up arresting somebody, and that would spoil Daddy's birthday."

Ryan rubbed his nose with the back of his index finger. "Okay, we'll take it outside."

"I'd rather you didn't," Diane told him.

Wade shifted his weight from side to side. "Come on, punk, what'll it be? You gonna let a girl tell you what to do?"

Ryan gave Diane an arched look. "You think I should let him get away with talking about my mother and me like that?"

"No, of course not."

"Come on, Diane, get out of the way. Let the little bastard try to take me on. I'll mop the floor with him."

"You and what army?" Ryan retorted.

"Just hold it," Diane shouted. "Look, Ryan, I know he's insulted you, but he would have insulted anyone I danced with. He's trying to embarrass me into going steady with him again, but I already told him I don't go with dopeheads."

"I ain't no dope—"

"And I told you not to ever come around me again while you were using, didn't I?"

"Hey!" Wade spread his arms wide. "I'm clean."

"Sure you are. That's why the whites of your eyes look like raw meat."

The eyes in question narrowed. "You listen here, you little—"

"What's—"

That was Jerry's voice, cut off in midbreath. Beth saw Carol with her elbow in her husband's ribs. When Luke would have stepped forward again, Carol cautioned him back with a look.

"You're not gonna call her a name, are you?" Ryan asked softly.

"That's okay," Diane said. "Let him."

Ryan shook his head. "But you said I couldn't hit him."

"That's right. You can't hit him, because it would start a brawl. You can't go out back, because then your uncle J.D. would have to arrest you for fighting. My daddy and your daddy can't hit him, because Wade's still a kid, even if he does act like a Neanderthal. So..."

"So," Wade said, "if nobody's gonna hit anybody, then dance with me."

Diane glanced over her shoulder and caught her mother's eye. Carol gave her a narrow-eyed nod. The girl turned back to Wade. "I didn't say nobody was going to get hit."

"Yeah, well, who's gonna get it?"

"You are."

"By who?" He spread his arms wide. "There's nobody left."

"There's me." Diane bunched her fist and connected a right swing to Wade's nose. Into the hushed silence that followed Wade's exclamation of pain and surprise, Diane said, "Get lost, creep."

After one long, startled silence, the room burst with sudden laughter. If Diane's punch wasn't enough to send Wade running, the laughter of his peers was. As he hit the bottom of the stairs on his way up, Jerry stepped into his path. "Don't ever bother my daughter again. You got that?"

But Wade didn't stop to answer. He barreled past Jerry and Carol, past both his stricken parents right behind them, and took the stairs two at a time, one hand clutched over his bleeding nose.

Within a very few minutes Beth and Luke, Carol and Jerry, and Diane and Ryan were behind closed doors in the master bedroom upstairs. Diane was using a bag of frozen corn as an ice pack for her knuckles. And she was grinning. So was her mother.

"Somebody wanna tell me what's going on?" Jerry stood fuming, glaring at his wife and daughter, his hands on his hips. "You two have been plotting again, haven't you?"

"Oh, cool off," Carol told him. "That creep has been bugging Diane for months. She wanted to handle this herself, and I'm damn proud of her." Carol put a hand on Ryan's shoulder. "And I want to thank you for letting her take care of him herself."

Ryan stuffed his hands into his pockets and shrugged. "Kinda went against the grain, you know? I mean, my mom taught me—"

"She taught you to take up for girls?" Luke asked,

intrigued at how cool Ryan had been during the whole scene.

"Yeah, but only if the girl needs it." Ryan grinned. "Diane didn't need it. Besides, Mom told me never to argue with my elders."

"Why, you—" Diane shrieked.

"Hey, I'm only telling the truth," Ryan cried with feigned innocence. "You said yourself you were a day older than me."

Diane looked as if she couldn't decide whether to punch Ryan or laugh. She ended up laughing, and so did the others.

When the others left the room, with Carol vowing to go yank Wade's mother away from the food table, Luke held Beth back. "Does he have to deal with that sort of thing often?"

Beth didn't pretend not to know Luke was concerned with Ryan being called a bastard. "No," she said, "not often." But even once was too often as far as she was concerned. In the past she had always blamed Luke for the label forced on her son. Now that she knew the truth, though, she could no longer do so. The blame lay solely on her own aching shoulders.

"I hate it, Beth," Luke said fiercely. "I hate the idea of anybody calling my son a bastard. Of him needing to defend himself."

"It doesn't thrill me, either. He's my son, too, Luke. He and I talked about all this a long time ago. He understands that it's no fault of his, and he deals with it the best he can."

"He shouldn't have to deal with it, dammit!"

"I know that," she cried. "But he does have to. Because of my grandmother's lies and my stupidity, he does. I was wrong to believe her, all right? I was wrong. When she offered to send me the picture of you and Carol out of the newspaper, I should have demanded she do just that. Instead, I got so sick at the thought of having to see it with my own eyes, I threw up. When she came to visit and tried to talk me into an abortion—"

"God, no."

"—I shouldn't have cared if you were married or not. I should have run screaming back to you. Instead, I nearly miscarried and ended up in the hospital. I screwed up your life, mine and Ryan's. I can't undo it, Luke. All I can do is try to live with it."

Luke grasped her shoulders and ached at the sight of her tears. "Beth, I wasn't blaming you."

"Weren't you?"

He hung his head and closed his eyes. In reality, he had harbored a tiny seed of resentment against her since learning the truth. He had blamed her for believing the lies, for not getting in touch with him. For not telling him about his son.

He'd thought he had let go of all that baggage when he overheard her talking to Carol in the grocery store earlier. Apparently he hadn't, because as he thought about what he'd just said to her, he realized how accusing he'd sounded.

But it didn't matter now. The past couldn't be undone, and he didn't want Beth to hurt anymore.

"If I were you," she said, "I'd blame me. I *do* blame me."

"Stop." He pulled her close, ignoring her efforts

to resist. "Stop, babe. Don't do this. No more blame. Please. No more. Get rid of it. Cry it out and let it go. No more looking back."

But Beth didn't cry, wouldn't let herself. She was still too rattled over everything that had happened that day with Luke and Ryan, even Carol. If she started crying now, she wasn't sure she'd ever stop. So she pasted on a smile, thanked Luke and led the way back out into the party.

Shortly after they emerged from the privacy of the bedroom, Beth was ready to go home. She said good-night to Carol and Jerry, and gave Jerry a final birthday hug. Luke walked Beth and Ryan the three doors to her father's house.

"I really admired your restraint tonight," he told Ryan. "I was proud of you."

Under the dim glow of the streetlight at the corner, Ryan flushed with the praise.

Beth said, "I was proud of him, too. He doesn't always show such good judgment."

"Meaning?" Luke asked.

"Meaning sometimes he comes home with swollen knuckles."

Luke looked at his son with a wry grin. "She's probably gonna kick me for this, but sometimes a fist in the mouth is the only thing a jerk like that guy tonight understands."

Beth gave Luke a tap on the shin with the toe of her sneaker. "Don't encourage him, for heaven's sake."

At the front door of her father's house, Luke made Beth face him. "Don't forget. You promised to think about the reunion."

Chapter Ten

Think about the reunion.

In the end, Beth barely thought of anything else all night and through the next day. Her father would want her to stay, her grandmother would want her to go. Beth had no idea what Margaret would say. Ryan was eating up all the attention from Luke and the rest of the Ryans, but did he miss his friends? Was he anxious to get home? On the way to bring her dad home from the hospital Sunday afternoon, she asked Ryan those questions.

He gave a shrug as though his answer weren't important, but she saw the sudden stiffening of his arms and shoulders. "I don't know. It's not up to me, is it?"

"No, but I'd like to know what you think."

"About staying here?"

"Maybe. For another couple of weeks."

"Could we?" There was no denying the wistful tone of his voice, even though he tried to hide it.

"You don't miss your friends?"

Another shrug. "Some, maybe. But this is different. This is family. Except for you and Gran and Grandma Rose when she visits, I've never had a family."

"And you kinda like it, huh?"

As Beth pulled in at the hospital, Ryan grinned. "Yeah, I like it a lot."

They got out of the car and started toward the door. Clouds were building up for the daily sprinkle that would last only a few minutes. "Are we staying, then?" Ryan asked.

"I don't know. Don't say anything to anyone yet. I'm not sure if I can get the time off work. If I can't, we'll have to go back."

"Maryjo? Hi, this is Beth."

"Beth," Maryjo said over the slight static of the phone line. "How is everything? How is your father?"

"He's better. As a matter of fact, he came home from the hospital yesterday."

"Wonderful. I know you must be pleased."

"Yes. Listen, is your husband around?"

"No, he stopped at the store on the way home. Anything I can help you with?"

"I don't know. I suppose I should talk to him, but..." Beth poked her finger into the coiled phone cord. "How do you think he'd feel about giving me another couple of weeks off? How would you feel about filling in for me that long? I wouldn't ask if it wasn't important."

"I know you wouldn't, Beth. Let's see." Maryjo chuckled. "How do I put this diplomatically? We miss you. He misses you at work, I know. But—now, don't take this wrong—I'm having so much fun working in the office again, as far as I'm concerned, you can take the whole summer off."

Beth laughed. "The whole summer, huh?"

"Without pay, you understand."

"Naturally." The whole summer. No, she couldn't stay the whole summer. But at least until the reunion. Maybe a little longer. Maybe. "How do you think Walt would feel about another three or four weeks?"

"Here he is now. Hang on."

Beth heard Maryjo explain, then Dr. Walt McKinzie took the phone. "You're trying to get me killed, aren't you?"

"How's that?" Beth asked.

"If I tell you to come back, Maryjo will think I'm insulting her work at the office. If I tell you to stay gone, you'll be insulted. What's a guy to do?"

Beth laughed. "Life is so tough, isn't it?"

"You're not kidding. But listen, if you need a few more weeks, that's fine. Maryjo will be available to fill in until school starts."

"Thanks, Doc, you're a pal." They visited a few more minutes, then said goodbye.

Beth's hand shook as she replaced the receiver in its cradle. She'd done it. She and Ryan were staying. But she would keep the time beyond the reunion to herself for now.

Before she lost her nerve, she dialed Luke's number.

Luke hung up the phone, then raised a fist in the air. *"Yes!"* he shouted to his empty house. Beth and Ryan were staying, at least for two more weeks. Beth would fill in at the clinic starting Wednesday. Luke would get to spend time with her and with their son.

Maybe now he would have the chance to figure out exactly what his feelings were for her. Were they only nostalgic? Was he merely trying to relive his youth? Or was he falling in love all over again, with the woman this time, instead of the girl?

Beth had fully anticipated suffering a severe case of nerves her first day at the clinic. Not that she was worried about the work—she knew she could handle it. What unnerved her was the idea of working with Luke.

It turned out she had worried for nothing. There simply wasn't time to be nervous; there was too much to do.

Three full-time physicians served the clinic and hospital. They worked two at a time on a rotating shift, twelve days on, nine days off. The two on duty took turns being on call at night. Next week the doctors would start giving physicals for the coming school year. On the average of every two and a half minutes the phone rang, someone wanting an appointment for the required physical.

Beth was knee-deep in getting organized when the first patient of the day arrived—Kat Ryan. It was time for another prenatal checkup, and J.D. had come with her.

"Beth," Kat cried. "What on earth are you doing here?"

"Saving the clinic's hide," Luke replied as he greeted his sister-in-law.

J.D.'s face lit. "Does this mean you're staying? You've moved back to town?"

"No," Beth said with a little catch in the vicinity of her heart. "No, I'm just filling in for a while, that's all. Just until they hire a new office manager."

Luke took Kat's arm. "Come on, Mama, let's go check out this baby. You coming, J.D.?" he asked over his shoulder.

J.D. rolled his eyes. "I don't think so."

"What? You're not gonna come watch me look up your wife's dress?"

Kat burst out laughing at the way J.D.'s eyes popped wide open.

"Now, Dr. Ryan," Betty, the nurse, said as she followed Luke and Kat into the exam room. "What a thing to say to your own brother. Don't give the poor deputy any more grief than he's already got. You know he almost didn't survive morning sickness."

J.D. stuffed his hands into his pockets and said to Beth, "And here I was hoping you'd have a steadying influence on him. He's still as ornery as ever."

Beth chuckled. "I can see that."

Then J.D. sobered. "I can't tell you how pleased we all are to have you back in town, and to learn about Ryan. But I have to tell you, I'm not sure Luke can survive you leaving again, Beth."

"J.D.—"

"I know, it's none of my business. I've said all I'm going to on the subject. Except—I think you're crazy to even think about going back to Missouri. This is your home. It always has been, always will be. End of sermon."

From a distance, never venturing from the relative and sometimes dubious security of her mother's house, Margaret watched what was happening with Beth and Ryan and Luke. Ryan came to visit Rose and her and told them about Beth filling in at the clinic. Neighbors spoke of seeing the new father-and-son team around town. Then, too, Margaret knew Leon was home from the hospital.

It was time to take a long, hard look at her life, Margaret decided. Time for some serious soul-searching. Time for the rest of the truth.

Once she confessed, Margaret knew she would lose everything. Her daughter, her grandson, even her own mother would turn against her, but for different reasons. And Leon. But then, Leon was already lost to her, had been for years. That was no one's fault but her own.

If she thought for a minute he would take her back, she would keep her mouth shut about her part in ruining so many lives. But there was no chance for her with her husband, and she didn't think she could live with the guilt any longer.

All she had to do now was work up the nerve to confess. Lord help her, she feared desperately that the truth was going to take more courage than she possessed.

* * *

By Friday afternoon Beth had worked at the clinic for three days. That was all it took for her to know she'd made a tactical error. She should never have agreed to fill in. She could have stayed in town without working, at least for a while. But no, she'd had to get involved. She'd had to go and grow attached to the place, the people.

She loved the small clinic where every patient was a neighbor, a friend. When Mrs. Long from the drugstore came in with a sprained wrist, Beth ached with her. When Gwen Greene's youngest daughter stepped on a rusty nail and had to have a tetanus shot, it was Beth who teased the girl's tears away and held Gwen's hand. When Janey and Terry Perini learned they were *finally* expecting their first child, Beth celebrated with them.

One after another they came—old friends, new ones—and Beth cared. She cared too much. How was she supposed to leave in a few weeks?

Then, too, there were her feelings for Luke. The feelings she didn't trust, the feelings she feared. As she straightened her desk Friday evening and picked up her purse to leave, she thought it was a damn shame no one had perfected the use of the crystal ball for the layperson. She would dearly love to be able to look into one and know what she was going to do.

"All through?"

Beth jumped at the sound of Luke's voice behind her. She put a hand to her chest and took a deep breath. "You scared the tar out of me."

"Sorry," he said with a slight grin. "I didn't mean to. I was just going to offer to walk you to your car."

"Thanks, but I didn't drive today. I walked."

Luke grinned. "Bet you don't do that in Kansas City."

"Bet you're right. The clinic is twelve miles from our house."

"Well, come on, then. I was headed out myself. I'll walk you home."

"You don't have to do that."

"I know, but I want to."

Dampness clung to the streets from the brief rain shower that had passed through earlier in the afternoon. Occasional drops still fell from trees, the grass glistened a deep emerald in the clear sunlight, and flowers sparkled as though bejeweled. The air was clean and sweet and cool. Beth took a deep breath. Nothing smelled quite so wonderful as desert mountain air after a rain.

"You really seem to have whipped things into shape at the clinic," Luke told her as he slowed his steps to match hers.

Beth laughed. "Considering you took me at my word that I knew what I was doing, you mean."

"Well." He smiled. "There is that. But I trusted you, the board trusted me. You're very good at your job."

She arched a brow. "You don't have to sound so surprised."

"Not surprised," he denied. "It's just a side of you I've never seen before, never thought about." When she didn't respond, he sobered and said, "We're different now, aren't we?"

"We're grown up, is that what you mean?"

"I guess." He gave a sad smile. "You used to need

me more, depend on me. Now you're so damned capable, so used to taking care of yourself, I guess you don't need anybody.''

''Why do you say that?'' He made her sound like a stranger to herself.

''Look at you, at your life.'' He gestured with one hand, then stuffed both hands into his pockets. ''You obviously didn't need me to raise our son. He's wonderful. You're a terrific mother. He's more well adjusted than most kids with two parents. You didn't need me to earn your way in the world. You know your business well. With your skills, you could earn a living anywhere you wanted to live. You say you've been happy, so you obviously haven't needed me for that.'' He lowered his head and hunched his shoulders. ''I don't even want to know about the men in your life. A woman like you could have any man she wanted.''

''I could say the same things about you.'' Beth met his gaze, then looked away as they passed her grandmother's street and kept walking. ''You don't look like you've been pining away all these years. You must have a flock of women after you.''

His only answer was a short, bittersweet laugh.

''So if we're both so wonderful and so happy,'' Beth said softly, cautiously, even a little unwillingly, ''why has neither one of us married?''

Luke halted at the base of the hill where the street leveled out. He turned to face her, and took her hand in his. ''Maybe we should explore that question.''

Beth swallowed at the intensity in his eyes. Her knees trembled. Her breath hitched and thinned. After so many days of backing away from him, did she dare let him close? "What did you have in mind?" Lord have mercy, she couldn't believe she'd said that.

"Let's cut to the chase, Beth. I know we can't pick up where we left off sixteen years ago, but something's still there between us. We both know it. I want to know if it has a chance. And if it does, are you willing to let us take it?"

The trembling in her knees spread to her middle. Heavens, was she supposed to be able to answer a question like that, after all that had happened to them? She looked away. "I know you said you didn't blame me anymore—"

"And I meant it," he interrupted. "I don't blame you, and I don't want you blaming yourself."

"Blame or not," she said, meeting his gaze while her eyes filled up, "I hurt you. By believing my grandmother, I hurt you, Luke."

"It doesn't matter anymore. That was then. This is now. Don't let what happened come between us anymore, Beth. Give us a chance."

Her mouth went dry and her heart knocked against her ribs. "What, exactly, are you suggesting?"

"That we start over and try again."

Her knees nearly gave way. "How?"

He gripped her hand more tightly. "Get to know each other, learn who we are now. Date. That sort of thing."

Beth covered her mouth with the back of one hand and looked away, blinking rapidly.

"Don't tell me you haven't been expecting this. Surely you didn't think we could just say hello, how are you, see you in another sixteen years."

"No. I didn't think that. It's just…all so scary, you know?"

He rubbed his thumb back and forth across the back of her hand. "What's scary?"

Somewhere close, a dog barked. Beth jerked, suddenly aware they were standing on the street corner in full view of anyone who cared to look. She pulled her hand from Luke's and started walking east on Bell toward her street.

Date. Good grief, he was asking her to date him. Date, and "that sort of thing." He could have no idea how scary that sounded to someone who hadn't been on a date in years, and hadn't done "that sort of thing" in even longer.

"Is it me you're scared of?" he asked quietly. "Am I that much of a stranger to you?"

The hesitancy in his voice drew her to look at him, at his familiar, gorgeous face, his familiar, deep blue eyes. "No," she answered. "I don't think of you as a stranger. But you were right, Luke. We don't really know each other any longer. We're different people."

"All I'm asking for, Beth, is a chance for us to do something about that, to get to know each other."

"I…" Why was she hesitating? She wanted this. What difference did it make if the thought of getting closer to him scared her? That was nothing compared to the thought of never knowing him again. "I'd like that."

Luke nearly buckled with relief. For an eternity there on the street, he'd feared she would tell him no, and he wouldn't have been able to stand it if she had. But she'd said yes. She'd said yes!

So now what, hotshot? How are you going to go about winning her back?

He didn't even question his own choice of words. He just went with them. "Good," he said. "How about dinner tomorrow night? I'll be on call, so we'll have to stay in town. Otherwise I'd suggest we go to Vernal for a movie."

Oh, God, so soon. Somehow she'd thought he might give her time to get used to the idea first. "You have to drive clear to Vernal these days for a movie?" she asked, hedging.

"Since they shut down The Derrick more than ten years ago."

"I wondered, but then I saw the video store."

"Yeah, that helps some, but it's not like having a theater. So how about dinner?" He waited, his breath held tight in his lungs. Waited, while the elm leaves dappled sunlight on her hair. Waited what seemed like forever before she spoke.

"Okay."

Okay. Everything was going to be okay. All she had to do was calm down.

Beth pressed her ice-cold hands against her fiery cheeks and stared at herself in the mirror on the dresser in her bedroom. It was only Luke, for heaven's sake, only a date with Luke. Just because she hadn't been on a date since her son was ten years old, that was nothing to be nervous about.

"The hell it's not," she said aloud. Five years between dates was plenty to be nervous about, in her book.

Through her closed bedroom door she heard someone knock on the front door. Panicked, she glanced at the clock. Her heart lodged in her throat. She wasn't ready! It couldn't be Luke! It was only four; he wasn't due until seven.

From the living room, her father called her.

Calm. She just needed to be calm, that was all. With a deep breath, she opened her door and went to see who'd arrived.

"Someone at the door for you." Her father looked suspiciously smug and way too cheerful for her peace of mind.

"Who is it?"

"Go find out."

Beth approached the front door with caution. She pushed the storm door open, then gaped at the young woman standing on the porch.

"Bethany Martin?"

Beth swallowed. "Yes."

"This is for you," the woman said with a smile.

"Oh, my." Beth's heart gave a little flip in her chest. "Thank you." With shaking hands she reached out and accepted the crystal bud vase bearing a single, perfect long-stemmed red rose. While she stared at it, the young woman backed off the porch and returned to the car she'd left idling at the curb.

Beth was oblivious to the eager stares of her father and son as she carried the rose into the house and placed it carefully on the coffee table before the sofa.

"Wow, Mom."

Yes, Beth thought. Wow, indeed. Only twice before in her life had anyone given her a rose. Once, about ten years ago, Ryan had plucked one from a neighbor's flower bed and brought it to her for Valentine's Day. It had been so sweet of him, and had cost him a hole in two fingers where he'd stuck himself with the thorns, that she'd cried and embarrassed him. The only other rose she'd ever received had also been on Valentine's Day, during her senior year of high school. It had been from Luke.

"Who's it from?" Ryan asked, leaning over her shoulder.

"Huh," her dad said, the smugness now in his voice. "Give you three guesses."

"Ho!" Ryan shouted. "You mean it's from my dad? Hey, Granddad. How 'bout that. Dad sent Mom a flower."

Not just a flower, Beth thought, but a rose. A beautiful, perfect rose.

"You gonna read the card?"

Beth shot her son a terse look. "Not with you leaning over my shoulder like that."

Ryan grinned, but he moved away. Beth unpinned the small florist's envelope from the yellow ribbon tied in a bow at the neck of the vase. Her hands shook as she pulled out the card.

Can't wait until seven. Yours, Luke.

"What's it say? Is it really from Dad? Come on, Mom."

Beth tucked the card back into the envelope and held it close. "What it says is none of your business. I'm going to go take a long, hot bath."

Ryan snickered. "With bubbles, probably, to get ready for your hot date."

In the end, there were bubbles in her bath. And at five minutes to seven Beth stood once again before the dresser mirror with her icy hands pressed against her fiery cheeks.

Yours, Luke.

But was he hers? Did she dare want him to be?

Luke pulled the Mark VII up to the curb in front of the Martin house and shut off the engine. Times had sure changed, he thought, amazed. He'd pulled up at this curb probably a hundred times in the past to pick Beth up for a date. Back then he'd been driving his dad's pickup. The floor mats had always smelled slightly of sheep dung. This time the interior of his vehicle smelled like new car.

And this time he wasn't a cocksure teenager coming to pick up his girl for a run up in the hills to a kegger at one of the oil wells. No, now he was a thirty-four-year-old doctor with sweaty palms and a pounding heart, coming to take a woman to dinner. A woman. Beth. The mother of his son. The only woman he'd ever loved.

Lord, have mercy.

Luke got out of his car and walked up the familiar cracked sidewalk, up the same two steps to the same small wooden porch he'd stood on countless times, and knocked on the same old door. When Leon opened it, déjà vu struck Luke in the chest. When he stepped into the living room and greeted his son, the feeling eased. A moment later, as Beth stepped into the living room from the hall, the déjà vu mixed with something new and knocked the wind out of him.

How many times had he stood on that very spot and watched her come through the door? Too many to count, too long ago to matter. Yet it did matter.

But even as he thought of old times, he realized this time was different. As he'd told her yesterday, they weren't the same people anymore. Oh, sure, parts of them were, but they had grown up, grown away from each other. They were strangers, yet they weren't.

Her hair hung loose and dark over her shoulders, looking like shiny satin in the evening light. Her skin glowed soft and golden, arms, shoulders and upper chest left bare to his gaze by the yellow sundress held up by no more than two thin strips of material no wider than a string of spaghetti. A slender gold chain hung from her neck to just below the slight knobs of her collarbone.

The yellow fabric of the dress molded itself to her torso and nipped in at her narrow waist. Luke's hands trembled with the need to touch. From her waist the dress hung in soft gathers to just above her knees.

Lord help him, her legs were bare. On her feet she wore delicate white sandals.

"Hi," she said.

His gaze traveled back up to her face, her beautiful, familiar face, more perfect with the added years than he would have thought possible. Her eyes held a smile and a hint of shyness. Her hands, he noticed, were fiddling with her skirt.

The revelation struck him that she was at least as nervous as he was. The idea soothed something inside him. He smiled back. "Hi. You look...sensational. Are you ready?"

Beth blew air from between her parted lips. Was she ready? He stood there in boots, starched jeans and shirt, looking not like a doctor, not like her high school sweetheart, but like every female's dream of a rugged cowboy hero, and he asked if she was ready? An hysterical giggle bubbled up in her throat. She coughed to disguise the sound and force it back down.

Chapter Eleven

He took her to The Last Chance for dinner. The name was different from what it had been years ago, but the place was familiar. Beth tried to remember what it used to be called, and couldn't. She didn't ask, because not remembering seemed...disloyal. She should have been able to remember.

The current name, however, made her wonder if Luke had brought her here on purpose. He'd asked that they give themselves another chance. Would it, indeed, be their last one?

On their way to an empty table near the back of the small dining room, Luke paused at nearly every table to say hello, ask about friends and family of those he spoke with. He deliberately included Beth in the conversations that took place over the music wafting from the jukebox in the front corner.

They finally made it to their table, and the waitress brought them each a menu. Not a standard menu, but a large, eight-page newspaper, which contained not only the menu, but old newspaper articles on the history of Rangely. One about the town being named for an English lord in 1881; the frontier hardships faced by doctors; an article from 1947 about the Rangely oil fields needing rescuing from a "sea of mud." Something about a coyote in 1901, and three paragraphs about the day fifteen hippies came through on the way to Washington, D.C., back in 1967.

While the stories intrigued her, Beth couldn't keep her gaze from straying to the man across the table. Her date. She peered at him over the top of the menu. "Thank you for the rose. It's beautiful."

Luke met her gaze. All they could see of each other over the papers they held was from the eyes up. "So are you," he said softly.

Flustered at the compliment—she wasn't used to compliments from men; hell, she wasn't used to dates, either—she lowered her gaze and tried to make sense of the words that swam before her on the "dinner" page.

Conversations buzzed around them. Flatware clinked against plates. Randy Travis sang on the jukebox. From beyond the door to the kitchen, pots and pans clanked, meat sizzled, someone cursed, then laughed. And at the table near the back corner the newspaper rattled in Beth's hands.

"I'm glad you liked the flower," Luke said.

Once more Beth met his gaze over the tops of their papers. The soft smile in his eyes soothed her.

"Do you get a lot of them?" he asked.

Beth folded her menu and put her hands in her lap.
"A lot of what?"

"Roses."

She smiled. "What a tacky question to ask a
woman."

"Yeah. You gonna answer it?"

She shook her head. "No, I don't get a lot of roses.
As a matter of fact, that's the third one I've ever
received in my life."

Luke folded his menu and tossed it to the empty
place on his right. "Since I know where you got the
first one and the last one, do I need to be jealous of
whoever gave you the second one?"

Luke? Jealous? What an intriguing idea. Then Beth
laughed and shook her head. "I doubt it. It was from
Ryan, when he was five."

The waitress returned. Luke ordered the sirloin, and
Beth settled on shrimp scampi. They talked about the
clinic, about Diane Howard showing Ryan around
town, about Leon grumbling because Luke wouldn't
sign the release to let him go back to work. When
Luke asked what she'd done on her day off, she told
him about Carol conning her into helping with the
upcoming reunion.

"She snared you, huh?"

"Yeah, but it's fun."

"So what's in the works?"

"Well, let's see." Beth looked at the ceiling in
thought. "We bought the last of the decorations today. We're having a catered dinner at the college,
then dancing at the Chevron Rec Hall. Nothing too
surprising."

Their meal arrived, and they talked about the ranch,

mutual friends, all sorts of things that weren't to the point, and they watched the sun set outside the west window of the small dining room. The one thing they did not discuss was where Luke expected this new chance of theirs, this dating, to take them. Where did Beth want it to go?

She would be lying if she said the possibility of moving back to Rangely hadn't crossed her mind. But it wasn't something she was ready to talk about. Even thinking about it scared her. Such a big risk, a big change, to consider rearranging her life and Ryan's, only to realize too late that what she and Luke were feeling was nothing more than a rush of nostalgia. She was glad he never broached the subject.

After the waitress cleared away their dinner plates, they lingered over coffee.

"What's Ryan doing tonight?" Luke asked.

"He and Diane were going to walk down to Chism's for burgers."

"Seems like those two kids are pretty thick all of a sudden."

Beth ran a fingertip around the rim of her coffee cup. "It does, doesn't it?"

"You don't sound too pleased about it," Luke noted.

Beth shook her head. "It's not that. I'm glad he's making friends, and Diane's a nice girl. I just..."

"Just what?"

She gave him a wry smile. "I just keep remembering us at fifteen."

Luke reached across the table and took her hand in his. "So do I, Beth." He squeezed her hand and wiggled his eyebrows. "Pretty hot stuff, huh?"

Beth hung her head and fought a laugh. Then she looked up at him and shook her head. "Yes. And now my—our—son is that age. It's scary."

As his smile softened, Luke gave her hand another squeeze. "Yeah, when you put it that way."

Their gazes lowered until both were looking at their clasped hands resting beside the salt and pepper shakers.

"Speaking of sons and fathers," Beth said, "don't forget to come for dinner as soon as you get off work tomorrow evening. Your dad will probably already be there. And I've invited Mr. Bower from next door. I hope you don't mind."

"Of course I don't mind."

"It's just that he's all alone, what with his kids scattered all over the country. I couldn't stand the thought of him spending Father's Day by himself."

Luke squeezed her hand gently and ran his thumb across her palm.

Beth shivered at the tingling sensation.

"You're right. Mr. Bower shouldn't be alone tomorrow. You're a nice person, Beth Martin."

"Well, thanks. I like you, too."

Luke sobered. "Do you?"

Flustered, embarrassed, Beth ducked her head. "Of course I do."

For long moments a thick bubble of silence seemed to surround them. Then Luke broke it. "This is nice," he said, letting her off the hook by changing the subject. "We never used to just sit together like this over a cup of coffee."

"We were always in too much of a hurry."

"Yeah." He ran his little finger across her palm.

The action shot tingles up her arm and down to her stomach, making her jerk. "So." She scrambled for something to say. "I was surprised to find out you live right across the street from my grandmother."

"I pretend she's not there."

"I don't blame you." She shook her head. "I just can't imagine you buying a house that close to her on purpose."

"I almost didn't. But I liked the house, so I decided not to pay any attention to her. We've managed to ignore each other quite well. In fact, until the night your dad asked for you, I'd never even been up her sidewalk, much less knocked on her door. You know, it's funny. I've hated that woman all these years, without even knowing what she'd done to us."

Beth looked down and studied the coffee in her cup. "Could we not talk about that tonight?"

"About what? About what she did, the lies she told? There's no point talking about it anymore, is there?" He caught her gaze, then looked away. "It's done. Sixteen years are gone, and we can't ever get them back. All we can do now is make sure that whatever happens next is what *we* want, not what she wants."

"Are we supposed to know what we want?" Beth asked quietly.

"I do."

He seemed so sure. She wanted to pick up her cup and take a sip of coffee—anything to stop the words bubbling in her throat—but her hands shook too hard. She would only spill the coffee. So the words fell from her lips, even though she was afraid of the answer. "What do you want, Luke?"

Without hesitation, without so much as a blink of indecision, his answer came. "You," he said simply. "I want you and our son, and I want us to have a life together. I want...everything, I guess."

"You make it sound so simple," she whispered. "So uncomplicated."

"Is it complicated for you, Beth?"

Lord, he had no idea. Was life complicated? Was the human heart? "Yes. And difficult," she admitted.

"Is there anything I can do to make it easier?"

"Yes. You could not rush me, not pressure me."

He gave her a wry grin. "I'll do my best, but don't think I'm going to sit back and let the next week slip by and calmly watch you drive right out of town without a fight."

His announcement shouldn't have startled her, not after his saying he wanted a life with her and Ryan, but it did. Startled her, and if she was honest with herself, the thought of him fighting to keep her thrilled her clear down to her toes, which were at that moment curled as tight as she could get them. Her own reaction unnerved her, made her want to bolt.

"You have to work tomorrow morning," she said. "Shouldn't we be going?"

Luke studied her a long moment, then reluctantly agreed. He paid the check, then held the door of the restaurant open for Beth to exit into the cool night air. In the car he thought about taking her to his house. Thought about it hard. She'd never been there, and he desperately wanted to see her in his home.

But she didn't want to be pressured. Hell, it had been only a day since she'd agreed to give them a chance. He had to give her time, not rush her some-place she wasn't ready to go. It was too soon.

Too soon, hell. It was sixteen years overdue.

Still, he didn't want her to feel rushed, and she was looking damn skittish over there hugging the car door as if she couldn't wait to get out, so at the stoplight he turned in the opposite direction from his house.

"Where are we going?"

He gave a one-shouldered shrug. "Just driving. Is that okay with you?"

"Oh. Sure."

Three blocks north of Main they passed the edge of town.

"What's out here these days?" Beth gestured toward the stretch of land that was maybe a half mile long between the last residential street and the White River at the base of the bluffs.

"You mean besides the river? The sewage treatment plant."

A bark of laughter escaped Beth. "You really know how to show a girl a good time, Doctor."

He shot her a teasing look. "Are you impressed yet?"

A moment later they passed the turnoff for the plant and kept going. Beth's laughter faded. She knew, Lord, she knew where he was taking her, but couldn't bring herself to object.

They crossed the river, and where the road split in a flat Y at the foot of the bluffs, Luke turned right. A moment later he left the pavement for a dirt-and-gravel road that wound up into the barren hills.

The hills were only barren on the outside, however. Down inside the shale lay part of the Rangely oil field. The town of Rangely had boomed and busted so many times over the years, always right alongside the price of oil. The last bust had been in the eighties, but, surprisingly, the town had not dried up and blown away. Times had been hard, but the town and its residents were surviving.

Dust billowed up behind the car as they took the dark, twisting road around and up, until they pulled out on top of a flat bluff. Spread out before them lay the White River directly at the base of the bluff, and beyond that, the Rangely basin, wide and dark, with only a smattering of lights to indicate the presence of man.

Man's presence was more than adequately represented, however, right there on the top of the bluff, by the giant, monster-sized oil well pump chugging away, pulling oil from deep beneath the ground. Well 12.

This wasn't the only well along the bluffs, by any means. There were numerous others, and more scattered all over the basin and in the hills to the south. But Well 12 was special to any Rangely teenager who'd ever gone parking or watched a romantic sunset or attended a kegger complete with free-flowing beer, the requisite bonfire and, inevitably, the cops to run them all home.

"I can't believe it's still here," Beth said with awe. "And still pumping."

"For more years than I can remember." Luke braked and slowed to let his headlights illuminate the base of the drab olive green pumper. "It's a new unit, though."

"I can tell. The old one was black and not so big, and a heck of a lot noisier."

Luke turned off the headlights and pulled on past the well to near the edge of the bluff, and parked. He cut the engine, and a deep quiet settled, barely broken by the sound of the pumper just yards behind them.

The only other sounds were of crickets singing, a chorus of frogs along the riverbank below, and the careful breathing of two people in the Mark VII who should have had a dozen things to say to each other, but suddenly didn't.

A half-moon lit the broad valley before them, its soft light pouring into the car and spilling across Beth's lap.

"I'm glad you—"

"I enjoyed—"

They spoke at once, stopped at once, then laughed nervously.

"What are we doing?" Luke asked with a rueful shake of his head. "I was going to say how glad I was you had dinner with me, and you were going to tell me how much you enjoyed it." He reached across the console between their seats and ran his hand down her bare arm until he covered her clasped fingers where they rested in her lap.

Beth felt the heat of his fingertips against her thighs through the thin cotton of her skirt. An answering heat stirred in the pit of her stomach.

"Hell, this is us, Beth." He gave her hands a slight squeeze. "We've known each other all our lives. We made a son together. Now we're acting like strangers."

She was afraid to turn and look at him, afraid of

being this close to him. It made her want things she wasn't prepared to deal with, like his arms around her, his lips against hers, her skin against his. "In many ways we are strangers," she said softly.

"And in many ways..." With the tip of one finger he touched her chin and turned her face toward his.

He was close. So close she could feel his breath against her cheek and see a sheen on his lips, as though he'd just moistened them. Her breath backed up in her throat.

"In many ways," he whispered again, his mouth coming closer, "we're not strangers at all."

Beth held her breath, waiting, anticipating, tasting before there was anything to taste. Then his lips brushed hers softly. Once. Twice. Her breath left in an audible sigh.

Luke whispered against her lips. "Beth. Oh, Beth." He claimed her mouth with his, slowly, gently, and it was sweeter than any memory he'd managed to hang on to over the years. His arms quivered with restraint as he reminded himself not to rush her.

Her lips parted, and his tongue took advantage and dipped between them, tasting, stroking, savoring. He forgot restraint, forgot everything but the woman in his arms as he pulled her close. God, he'd dreamed of this, of someday holding her again. The vision had tormented him for years. He'd denied it, cursed it, and her, every step of the way. But now...now he was living it. She was here in his arms. He was kissing her, and she was kissing him back. And whether she knew it or not, she was his.

Suddenly she winced and jerked away. He spent a long, foggy moment staring at her closed eyes and open mouth, watching the rapid rise and fall of her breasts as she gulped air into her lungs. Then he saw the way she massaged her side with her fingertips, and he realized what he'd done. He'd held her too tight, tried to pull her too close, and the damn console between their seats had gouged her ribs.

"I'm sorry," Luke said softly.

"It's nothing."

"Guess these seats just don't compare to that big one in Dad's old pickup, huh?" He'd thought to get a laugh from her, or better yet, some hint of yearning on her face. Instead, she looked...uneasy.

"Guess not." Beth had never felt so awkward and out of her depth in her life. Not even the first time Luke had brought her up to Well 12 so many years ago. Then, she'd been sure of herself and of him, and eager to experience whatever Luke wanted to show her. Lord, how she had loved him back then.

Now she was a grown woman, not a green girl. She had a nearly grown son. She was parked on a deserted hilltop with the man who'd given her that son, and she didn't have the slightest idea how to act.

"Come here." With a hand beneath each arm, Luke lifted her and maneuvered until she sat on his lap with one shoulder pressed tight against his chest, the other guarded closely by the steering wheel and both her legs draped over the console, leaving her feet in the seat she had just occupied.

"What are you doing?" she cried, breathless and startled.

"Something I've wanted to do since the day I walked into your father's hospital room and saw you standing there. No, longer than that. Sixteen years longer.'' He tilted the steering wheel up as far as it would go, then gently wrapped both arms around Beth and pulled her close. "I'm holding you."

The softness of his tone settled deep inside her and melted the tension that had been holding Beth rigid. She flowed against him and, with a breathy sigh, dropped her head to his shoulder.

"God, it feels good to hold you like this," he whispered, his nose nuzzling her ear. "I can't tell you how good."

They sat in silence for long moments. Nothing stirred but the wind, the pumper nearby and the careful breathing of two people whose bodies whispered that they never should have been separated.

Oh, Luke, it feels good to me, too, and I was so afraid it wouldn't.

Suddenly she felt him pull one arm from around her and fumble against the door panel.

"This seat does have one advantage over the old pickup." His teasing grin flashed in the moonlight.

The soft whine of a small motor stung the silence. As Luke's grin widened, the seat slowly tilted backward until Beth found herself lying prone across his chest.

"There." With a satisfied sigh, he replaced his arm around her shoulder and tucked her head beneath his chin. "That's better."

Beth felt her pulse quicken even as she relaxed more fully against him. He wasn't rushing her, pushing for something she wasn't ready to give. He was merely holding her, and oh, God, it felt good to be held by a man, by this man.

"Something's missing. Hold on." He pushed the

button on the door panel again and the seat rose upright. Then he touched a couple of buttons on the dash. By the time he started tilting the seat back again, a deejay from more than a thousand miles away announced that it was "time for The Drifters, from your favorite oldies station, KOMA, in Oklahoma City, 1520 on your dial."

Beth smiled. "When you go down memory lane, you don't miss a beat, do you?"

"How's that?"

"Same old parking spot, same ol' radio station, same ol' songs."

"You don't like it?"

"I didn't say that."

With a knuckle to her chin, Luke tipped her face toward his and kissed her. And caught fire. Her taste, the smell of spring flowers in her hair and on her skin, the precious feel of her weight against him, all assaulted his senses and left him reeling.

Beth didn't even think to resist, couldn't have if she'd tried. Feeling the heat rush through her veins was so glorious, so...liberating, she reveled in his kiss. For the first time in more years than she cared to remember, she felt desire curl hot and sweet in the pit of her belly.

Her fingers found his thick, soft hair and threaded through it over and over. Her heart pounded against his chest. Her lungs fought for air. Her tongue danced with his as their lips mated. Low and deep, her body quickened, moistened. She was astounded at how fast it was happening, but had no desire to slow things down. Not now. It felt too good.

Luke held her tighter, closer, as close as he could,

but it wasn't close enough. He ran his hands over her, feeling firm flesh beneath thin fabric. Over back and waist, hips and thighs, he caressed her. Then he touched smooth, bare skin above the back of her dress, over her shoulder, down her arm. Soft. Silky. Sleek as satin.

An ache bloomed in his chest, a sweet yearning to relearn all of her, every delicious inch. To know her again with his hands, his eyes, his mouth, his body. This was Beth. His dream. The dream of holding her, loving her, that he had buried so deep for so long, he had actually convinced himself over the years that he hated her.

All it had taken had been one look, there in Leon's room, for him to know he'd merely been lying to himself.

Beth, Beth.

The skirt of her dress hitched beneath his hand until he felt the smooth flesh of her thigh beneath his fingers. He felt her indrawn breath at his touch. Blood rushed to his loins, making him heavy, hot, hard. His body's reaction brought a moan to his throat.

He was skimming one hand up her thigh and pulling the thin strap of her dress off her shoulder with the other when the shriek of a police siren from less than twenty feet away blasted the stillness of the night.

Beth bolted up and hit her head on the top of the car. Luke fumbled for the button to raise the seat upright and cursed a blue streak as a spotlight sliced through the darkness directly into their eyes.

A tinny-sounding voice blasted through a loudspeaker with enough force to be heard in the next county. "All right, you two, this is the Sheriff's Department. Let's come up for air and take it on home."

Chapter Twelve

The siren cut off, to be replaced by the crunch of footsteps on gravel and deep, full-throated, booming laughter.

"Dammit," Luke called, shielding his and Beth's eyes from the glare of the spotlight and surreptitiously pulling her skirt back down over her thighs. "Knock it off, J.D.!"

With her face buried against Luke's neck, Beth didn't know whether to feel frustrated, appalled, angry, amused, or embarrassed. She found she was a little bit of each. Amid the tangle of emotions, she felt a bubble of tension-relieving laughter threaten to break loose.

Luke squeezed her arm and spoke low into her ear. "Don't you dare laugh. I'm gonna kill him for this."

But Beth heard the laughter in Luke's voice.

The beam from a flashlight bounced in time with J.D.'s approaching footsteps. Beth wondered how he could have managed to drive right up next to them, park the car and get out, without her or Luke hearing him. Then she remembered the kiss and thought it was no wonder they hadn't heard. It was a miracle, now that she thought about it, that they'd even heard the siren.

Still laughing, J.D. braced a forearm over the passenger door of the Lincoln and leaned down into the window. "You two kids playing doctor?"

Luke was too furious to appreciate the humor. His anatomically impossible suggestion to his brother drew a strangled gurgle from Beth. She better not laugh. She just damn sure better not.

"Now, now." J.D. grinned like a braying jackass. "What would your patients think of such language, much less the nice young lady sitting on your lap?"

Luke gave a sickly smile. "I think my patients would like the nice young lady sitting right where she is."

"Funny. Real funny. I just knew you had a sense of humor." J.D. winked at Beth. "What'd he do to get you up here, tell you it was his turn to watch for UFOs?"

Beth lowered her gaze and worked her mouth. Her fingers dug hard into Luke's neck, hard enough to make his wince. Her ribs shook against his. The whole scene was too disgusting for words. All Luke could think was, she just damn sure better not laugh.

J.D.'s laughter was bad enough. It made Luke grind his teeth while trying not to snarl audibly. Especially infuriating was that J.D. couldn't seem to stop.

J.D. gave the roof of the car a hard thump with the flat of his hand. Still laughing, he said, "Now, you two kids better get on outa here before I feel obliged to go tell your daddies what you've been up to. No telling what kind of trouble you could have gotten into if I hadn't come along when I did." He cracked up again. "Oh, Lord, wait till the guys hear about this."

"J.D.," Beth cried. "You wouldn't!"

J.D. laughed harder. "Lord, Lord, you oughta see the looks on your faces."

"J.D." Luke shot him the finger.

Beth made another one of those strangled squeals against Luke's neck.

J.D. shook his head and hooted. "Watch out, boy. I'm still an officer of the law."

"You're an idiot, is what you are. You breathe one word of this, so help me—"

J.D. cackled and doubled over to clutch his sides. "Oh, I'm gonna love having something to hold over your head for the next ten years."

"That's blackmail."

"Ain't it just?"

"Get lost, J.D."

"I'm going, I'm going. But don't you two be doing anything I wouldn't do, you hear?" With his shoulders shaking, J.D. turned and hooted all the way back to his car.

"I'm gonna kill him," Luke muttered.

Beth bit back a grin and crawled over the console into the passenger seat. Luke shook his head slowly several times, as if he simply couldn't believe what had just happened.

He started the car, and when they were halfway down the hill, Beth lost control and started laughing. At the glare Luke tossed her, she laughed harder. Before they reached the pavement at the base of the bluffs, Luke, too, was laughing.

"Talk about ruining a mood." He pulled up at the stoplight at Main and tried to stop laughing, but couldn't quite manage it. "God, I wanted to kill him."

Beth hugged her aching sides and tried to catch her breath. "You looked like you were ready to do just that. Oh, Lord." Beth heaved a sigh and wiped the tears from her eyes. "How embarrassing."

"Oh, I don't know." Luke grinned. "Tell the truth. When was the last time the law caught either one of us making out where we shouldn't be?"

"I don't know about you, but for me it was at that same damn well."

"And we were together."

"Yes," she said softly.

The light turned green. "Are you in a hurry to get home?" he asked.

Her answering shrug was noncommittal.

Luke reached across the console and took her hand. "Good."

Less than two minutes later Luke pulled up in his driveway and got out, then went around and opened her car door. "Come on. Let's go inside."

Beth hesitated. A trace of laughter remained in his eyes, but the heat from their kiss on the hill still glowed there, too. She even felt it inside herself, still flickering, threatening to singe her. If she went inside with him, she knew what would happen. What she didn't know was whether or not it was smart of her to let it. "Luke…"

"Come on." He tugged gently on her hand. "Just for a few minutes, at least."

Beth wanted more than anything to go into his house, to see where he lived, see the things he chose to keep closest to him. To see where he slept.

But it wouldn't be for just a few minutes. If she went inside with him, she knew, by the look in his eyes, the tension in his hand and the yearning in her own heart, that they would pass the dating stage and move on to "that sort of thing."

She wanted to take that step with Luke, she realized. Wanted it wholeheartedly, completely, with her body, mind and soul. She wanted to make love with him.

"Beth?"

She gave him a tremulous smile and stepped from the car. As he led her up the sidewalk to his front door, she asked, "How long have you lived here?"

"About six years." He opened the door and motioned her inside.

The living room was large yet cozy, dominated by a brown sofa more than six feet long. Long enough for Luke to stretch out on. A glass-topped oak coffee table sat before it, flanked by two forest green easy chairs. Soft light came from the lamp on the end table between the sofa and the far chair.

There was a fireplace along the back wall, bookcases along the west, with a desk angled in the corner. Walls in eggshell white and plush carpet of pale gray kept the room from being too dark.

It was a masculine room, yet not too much so. It

was a room Beth could be comfortable in. "It's nice," she said.

"It's empty," came his soft reply.

Beth met his gaze, knowing full well he didn't mean that the room or house suffered a lack of furnishings.

He took her hands in his and urged her close. "Or it was, until you walked in." He leaned closer.

Beth's knees trembled. More nervous than she'd been all night, she backed away. "Why don't we sit down?" she said with forced brightness.

She headed for the nearest chair at the end of the coffee table, but Luke took her elbow and guided her to the couch. "Now." He put his arm around her and pulled her close. With a hand to her chin, turning her face toward his, he said, "Where were we before that damn siren went off?"

Beth told herself they needed to slow down. She hadn't felt that way in the car up on the hill, but here in his home, things were different. Things could get out of hand too easily. They were already moving ahead way too fast. Why had she come in with him? Why had she thought she could do this?

But his lips were coming closer, full and firm and oh, so irresistible. She met them with her own and let out a soft sigh. It was just a kiss, after all. What was there to worry about? Just a simple little kiss.

A simple kiss...with complications, like the warm taste of his lips, the exquisite feel of his fingers threading through her hair, the arousing touch of his hand along her ribs, the comfort and rightness of his broad, firm chest.

Complications. Like the way her blood caught fire

at the sound of his low groan of satisfaction. The way her hands shook as she cupped his face. The way her heart and body cried out for more while her mind warned her he might only be feeling old feelings for a girl who no longer existed.

Complications. The kind that had Luke shifting until he lay stretched out on the couch, his head resting on a throw pillow, and Beth stretched atop his length like a lazy cat.

And while she tried to be logical, tried to analyze the situation to see if she was getting in too far over her head, to see if the kiss was taking her where she feared to go, one of Luke's hands slid up under her skirt.

"Now I remember," he whispered against her lips. "This hand was right about here." He slid the hand in question farther beneath her skirt until it rested on the back of her thigh, just shy of touching her panties.

Beth shivered at the warmth spreading across her skin from his palm.

Luke nipped at her lips. "And this hand was just reaching for..." The fingers of his other hand traced one thin strap over her shoulder. Traced and toyed with and tugged until the strap dangled down over her upper arm and the front of her dress sagged so low, one breast was all but revealed.

She moved against him, and Luke welcomed the flash of heat in his loins, the instant hardness. As badly as he wanted to keep his lips on hers, he also wanted—needed—to taste more of her. He trailed hot, openmouthed kisses down her neck and across to her smooth bare shoulder. With his cheek testing the soft fullness of her half-bare breast, Luke felt her heart pound and he held on tight. "Does this feel as right to you as it does to me?"

"Yes," came her breathless reply. "It feels right. You feel right."

Luke tensed at her tone. "Do I hear a 'but' in there?"

She braced a forearm across his chest and rose to look down at him. The lamplight shining behind her head haloed her. Her position also let the loose side of her dress fall even farther. Luke's breath lodged in his throat as one dusky nipple, aroused and hardened, peeked above the fallen fabric. He swallowed and forced himself to meet her gaze.

"But," she said softly, her expression earnest, "are we about to do what we're about to do because it's right for who we are now, or are we caught up in old times, trying to relive our youth?"

He threaded his fingers through her hair from scalp to ends, over and over, letting the silken feel of the dark strands send sharp tingles from his hand to the base of his spine. "Part of it's old times," he admitted with a crooked smile. "With our history, it would have to be. I don't ever want to forget the way it was between us back then. But part of it's new, too, Beth. After you left with your mother, I remember wishing we hadn't wasted all those years by waiting until those last few weeks to make love."

The memories darkened her eyes. "We said we'd wait until we got married."

"Then your mother started talking about sending you to college. I wish I'd been noble enough to urge you to go, to promise you I'd wait."

"I didn't want to go. I wanted you."

"I know, babe. I wanted you, too."

"So we stopped waiting."

"And right after that, you were gone. And I was just selfish enough to wish we'd never waited at all, that we'd taken what we wanted years earlier. If all I was going to have of you was memories, I wished I'd had more of them. I don't want to live on memories anymore, Beth, and I don't want to wait any longer."

Beth tried to smile, but couldn't. It was all she could do to keep her tears from falling. For her life, she couldn't remember a single reason she'd been hanging on to her caution. No more. He was right. They'd wasted too much time. Sixteen years too much. "Have I told you lately, Dr. Ryan, that I love you?"

His eyes went dark, his arms tense. "No." His Adam's apple bobbed up, then down. "As a matter of fact, you've never told Dr. Ryan you loved him. You told some kid once, a long time ago, but when a kid grows up and becomes a man, he still needs to hear it."

"When a girl grows up, she needs to hear it, too."

"Oh, God." Luke crushed her to his chest and wrapped trembling arms around her. "God, Beth, don't ever think for a minute I don't love you. I love you so much I ache with it." He scattered frantic kisses across her eyes, her cheeks, her lips. "I knew the minute I walked into your dad's room and saw you that first day that I'd never stopped loving you. Not for a day. Not for a heartbeat."

In a fury of long-denied yearning, mouth found mouth, large hand found firm breast, breath hitched and stopped. And two hearts that never should have been separated reunited and thundered together in celebration.

Beth felt the heat, that glorious heat only he could generate, gather down below her belly. Fingers of flame fanned out to engulf all of her.

His voice cracking with emotion, Luke whispered roughly in her ear, "I've missed you. I've missed you so damn much for so damn long."

Beth's heart constricted. "And I you," she whispered fiercely.

Luke couldn't get enough of her. Greed and urgency led his hands over hair and skin and fabric again and again. He took her mouth with his, desperate to fill the empty years with the heady taste of her. But not just her mouth. He wanted to taste all of her, every single inch of her perfect flesh.

On a groan, he tore his lips from hers and trailed them down her jaw. Twisting, shifting, he maneuvered until they lay stretched out on their sides, facing each other, with her back pressed against the back of the couch.

He trailed his kisses lower, beyond her collarbone, her moan of pleasure fueling the fire in his veins. Lower still, along the slope of her breast until he found the nipple that had taunted him only moments ago. Her breathless gasp as he laved the bud filled his head.

Sweet. She tasted sweeter than any candy, felt hard against his tongue. When he took the bud into his mouth and suckled, her fingers stabbed into his hair and held his head tight against her. Deep inside him, the knot of wanting twisted tighter.

With one hand he traced the smooth skin above her

knee. His eager palm slid up the back of her thigh until he reached elastic and lace and slipped beneath to cup the core of her heat. To give himself more room, he pushed his thigh between hers. His fingers found her slick heat and delved into her tightness.

"Luke." Her gasping cry echoed in his mind.

With a final nip, he left her breast and raised his head to look at her. The sight of her, neck arched, eyes closed, mouth open and struggling for air, pushed him closer to the edge of the flames.

She squirmed and tried to push his hand away.

"Easy, babe, just go with it."

"No," she cried. "I want you with me."

Luke flexed his fingers and felt her muscles tighten. "Look at me."

Slowly her eyes opened, turbulent and dark with arousal.

"You gave me your body, your virginity. You gave me a son. But hindsight tells me I've never given you a climax."

"Luke…"

"Let me, Beth. I was the first in so many ways for you. I wanted to be the first to give you this, too, but…let me give it to you now."

"I want you with me."

He tasted her lips again. "Next time." With his thumb he found the spot that sent her reeling.

The pleasure on her face was so intense it made his chest ache and sent a ball of fire pulsing into his loins. She was so responsive. A final stroke, and she flew for him, her release shattering, humbling, more arousing to watch than anything he could imagine.

His own need clawed at him, but he tamped it down and held her, cushioning her fall back to earth.

Her heart thundered next to his. When she finally opened her eyes, they were crystal clear and smiling. "I've always heard doctors were good with their hands. Now I know what they mean."

He laughed outright, her humor surprising him. "Liked that, did you?"

Her eyes narrowed. "You're not getting another word out of me."

"Yeah, well, I have in mind something else I've never given you."

She nipped at his lips. "What's that?"

Fighting the nearly crippling ache in his loins, Luke pushed himself up and lifted her in his arms. "A bed." He searched her gaze for acceptance and found it in the light in her eyes.

He didn't make it halfway to his bedroom before he had to taste her lips again. When their tongues mated, he closed his eyes and made it the rest of the way to his bed on what had to be sheer instinct, because his brain was shutting down, oblivious to anything and everything but the woman in his arms.

When he stood her beside the bed and undressed her, she turned shy. More shy than she'd been when they were teenagers. When she didn't reach to undress him, he told himself he wasn't disappointed.

He reached to unbutton his shirt, and she seemed to change her mind. Her hands pushed his away. "Please, let me."

The light touch of her fingers burned his flesh. He felt his back grow damp with sweat from the heat. When his shirt slid off his arms and her hands splayed across his chest, his knees started trembling. When her lips brushed across the skin over his breastbone, he sucked in a sharp breath and closed his eyes, his heart threatening to pound its way right out of his chest.

"When I was a boy," he managed, his voice shaking, "you made me feel like a man." He cupped her head in hands that weren't quite steady and lifted her face to meet his kiss. "Now I'm a man, and you make me feel like a kid again. My heart's pounding and my hands are shaking, and if I don't..." He had to stop to swallow, to catch his breath over the way her fingers trailed down his sides.

"If you don't?" Her voice was low and soft, her smile teasing.

And he'd thought her shy? He laughed roughly, half embarrassed at how far gone he was. "I've still got my damn jeans on and I'm not sure I'm going to last long enough to get them off."

Her eyes darkened, sending his blood pulsing hotter and harder into his aching loins. Her chuckle was pure torture, of the exquisite, feminine kind that had been driving men over the edge since Eve and her damn apple. Just as it was driving Luke nearer and nearer the edge now.

"Well..." She reached for the button at the top of his fly. Her cool fingers against his stomach made his muscles quiver. "We can't have that, can we?"

He wasn't going to make it. If he felt those fingers on the part of him that was ready to burst, he'd be finished before he started. With a low growl he tossed her onto the bed, yanked off his boots and shucked the rest of his clothes, then followed her down.

She welcomed him with open arms and cradled him between her silken thighs. But not yet, he told himself, not yet. Not until she was as wild for him as he was for her.

With hands and lips, teeth and tongue, he explored her face, her neck, her shoulders. Her breasts seemed to swell to fit perfectly in his palms. He tasted their tips and was gratified by her groaning response.

Her legs shifted alongside his. "Luke, please," she whispered.

That fast, she was ready for him, hot and slick again. Just as he was ready to sink himself into her depths, reality struck him. "Oh, damn. Wait. Beth, look at me."

He waited, his chest heaving for air, until she forced her eyes open and met his gaze. "Are you using any kind of birth control?"

With a moan of frustration, she closed her eyes and rolled her head from side to side. "No."

"Okay." He kissed her lips, her chin. "It's okay, I'll take care of it."

"Luke!" she protested as he moved off her.

"Wait. I'm sorry. Wait." With more willpower than he knew he had, he reached toward the floor for his wallet in the hip pocket of his jeans. When he found it, he flipped it open and pulled out a condom. With a wry grin, he said, "I'd have a hell of a time explaining to your father that I'd gotten you pregnant again."

Her smile wobbled. "We both would. Thank you."

He put on the condom, then rolled back into her arms. "Now, where were we?"

With eyes darkened with passion, Beth reached down and guided him. "Here. We were here."

And then he was there, sinking into her. She was tight. Achingly, exquisitely tight. Virgin tight, though he knew that was impossible. He shuddered with the need to bury himself completely in one swift thrust. But he couldn't hurt her, wouldn't.

"All of me," he whispered desperately. "Take all of me. Please."

Beneath him, she moaned. Her knees lifted higher. Her inner muscles rippled and urged him on until he was buried to the hilt. "All right?" he asked, his arms quivering as he held most of his weight off her.

"Yes." She moved beneath him. "Oh, yes."

Her breathless whisper threatened his control. Her hands on his back, sliding down to his hips, tore holes in it. The movement of her hips ripped it to shreds.

"I love you," they said in unison. "I love you."

Together they moved, mouths and hands and bodies melding in the heat, minds blending, souls soaring. An ancient, primal rhythm gripped them both, starting slow and strong, growing faster, harder, on and on, blazing hotter, searing them, sending them up, higher, higher still, until Beth dug her nails into his shoulders, her body convulsing beneath and around him.

The breathless cry of his name on her lips sent him straight over the edge.

Beth stretched her tender muscles and buried her nose in the wiry-soft hair on Luke's chest. Never, never in her life had she spent a night like this one. Not even close. "Luke?"

"Mmm?"

She grinned. He sounded so damn pleased with himself, like a cat who'd just copped the last mouse. "I have a confession to make."

He ran a lazy hand down her spine and cupped her backside. "Oh, good." He pulled her up until their faces were even and gave her a slow, heated kiss. "I like confessions."

"I don't know," she told him. "I'd hate to have your ego get out of hand."

"Oh? This confession is going to give me a swelled head?"

"Or something."

He chuckled. "Sounds interesting."

She ducked her head and nestled against his smooth, firm shoulder. "Remember earlier when you said you wished you'd been the first to...well, you know."

She felt his chest vibrate with another chuckle. "The first to what, Beth?"

"You were, you know. The first, I mean."

He went perfectly still for a long moment, then tilted her head up and searched her eyes intently, all teasing gone. "What are you saying?"

She swallowed. "The first, the second and the third. All tonight."

His eyes widened with amazement. "You're not serious." His brow came down in a frown. "My God, you are serious. You're thirty-four years old, and until tonight, you've never—"

"That's right."

"Why? How? What the hell's the matter with the men in Kansas City? No. Don't answer that. I don't think I want to know about the men in your life."

Beth gave him a wry smile. "The answer to your first two questions is in your last sentence. There haven't been any men in my life."

Tension sprang up fast and thick around them. "You can't mean...none?"

Oh, damn. She glanced away from those startled blue eyes. Why had she started this conversation? "One, a long time ago, and it was a disaster."

Luke stared at her a long moment, then let his eyes sink closed. He swallowed past the sudden tightening in his throat. No wonder she'd been as tight as a virgin. "Thank God you didn't tell me sooner. I would have been so intimidated I probably would have ruined the entire night for both of us."

Her soft breath trickled across his chest with her laughter. "I somehow doubt that. I'd think it would have been worse if you thought I might be comparing you to other men. Why should no men in my past intimidate you?"

He gazed at her solemnly. "I don't know, it just would have. I wanted everything to be perfect for you, but I would have been worried about—"

She cut his words off with a kiss. "It was perfect." Against her lips she felt him grin. "All three times," she added.

"You've been deprived, woman. Let's make it four."

Beth shuddered with pleasure. "By all means."

In the little white house on Stanolind, Leon Martin lay in bed with his hands clasped behind his head and stared at the glow of the streetlight on his ceiling, listening for the familiar squeak of the front door telling him Beth had come home. He'd been listening for the sound since around midnight when Ryan had finally turned off the television and bedded down on the sofa for the night. Listening in vain.

The only sound Leon heard, other than the creaks and groans of the old house as it settled, was that of his old windup alarm clock ticking the night away on his nightstand. The ancient glow-in-the-dark dial read 2:20. Leon knew it was accurate to the minute.

With a sigh he closed his eyes. The later the night got, the longer his daughter stayed out with Luke, the bigger Leon's smile grew. The greater his hope. If Luke Ryan was half the man Leon knew him to be, Bethany and Ryan Martin would not be going back to Kansas City.

Leon chuckled quietly into the darkness. He should probably be ashamed of himself. What self-respecting father wished his daughter was being seduced?

Chapter Thirteen

Sunday evening Margaret Martin stood at her mother's kitchen window with the curtains pulled aside and watched Luke Ryan get into his car and back out of his driveway. She'd seen him walk home from the hospital just twenty minutes ago, and now he was leaving. Unless he'd changed a great deal over the years, she was willing to bet that gift-wrapped package he'd carried with him to the car was a Father's Day gift for Zach, and Luke was on his way to the ranch.

Father's Day. The first one ever when Luke even knew he was a father.

What have I done to you, Luke? What have I done to all of us?

She knew instinctively that Ryan would be spending this evening with his father, too.

"What are you doing?" Rose demanded. "Let go of those curtains."

Margaret ignored her mother and stared out the window. Unless she missed her guess, Luke would take Ryan to the ranch with him, because Ryan would have already spent all day with Leon. That would leave Leon, and maybe Beth, at home.

"It's time," she whispered.

"Time for what?" Rose gave her a look of disgust. "Time for you to finally put on something other than that nightgown and robe you've been wearing all week? Time for you to quit sulking? Or, heaven forbid, time for you and Beth to go home where you belong?"

Margaret dropped the curtains and brushed a hand down the delicate nylon peignoir set. "Time for a lot of things." She raised her head and met her mother's glare. Funny, but Margaret had never noticed until lately that her mother always glared. "It's time," Margaret said slowly, "for the truth."

At first Rose looked startled. Then she shook her head and smiled sadly. "You'll never do it. You haven't got the backbone, dear."

That much, Margaret knew, was true. Never in her life had she had so much as an ounce of courage. It was time she learned.

Father's Day. Perhaps it was appropriate that she confess on this day. Her gift to Leon would be the truth.

And the truth shall make you free.

But not for Margaret, she knew. Her cowardice had cost her her husband years ago. Today, the truth would cost her her daughter.

* * *

In the privacy of his mother's bedroom Ryan wiped his sweaty palms down the thighs of his jeans. Did he have everything? Three cards. No, four counting the one for Mr. Bower his mom had insisted they get. The new wallet for Granddad because his was falling apart, the new pipe for Grandpa Zach, the new tackle box for Dad, the gnarled chunk of piñon for Mr. Bower.

Jeez, he'd never realized what a scary thing Father's Day could be. Scary, but...good. Because for the first time in his life he had not only a father, but two grandfathers, as well. Even the old guy next door, Mr. Bower, was kind of like an honorary grandfather, even if he did forget things now and then. Heck, what was a little memory problem when with a flick of a knife the guy could turn plain ol' chunks of wood into quail and hawks and robins and rabbits and deer and bears and mountain lions and horses and who knew what else?

Ryan was glad Mom had invited Mr. Bower. She said the guy's kids were grown and gone and never came to see him anymore. Ryan couldn't imagine knowing you had a father who wanted you, and not going to see him.

The door swung open behind him. "How's it going?" his mom asked.

Ryan eyed the row of presents and cards lined up on the bed. "I guess I've got everything."

"So, what do you think?"

He knew what she was asking. What did he think about finally getting to do something on Father's Day except pretend it was just an ordinary day.

He stuck his hands in his back pockets and

shrugged. "It's like Christmas, only I get to do all the giving. It feels...neat."

Beth smiled softly at her son. How could she even think of taking him away from his father and two grandfathers, now that he'd found them? And after last night...

Voices from the front room told her their guests were arriving. "Come on, kiddo, let's go."

Zach arrived first, then Mr. Bower from next door, then Luke. Mr. Bower looked slightly abashed at being included at the special dinner, but it was Luke whom Beth watched, for it was Luke whose eyes were the hungriest when they settled on Ryan.

Ryan's eyes glowed when he looked at his father and said, for the first time in his life, "Happy Father's Day."

A huge lump rose instantly to Beth's throat.

Luke's smile was huge and shy and a little unsteady. "Thanks." Then he chuckled at Ryan. "Does this feel as strange to you as it does to me?"

Ryan laughed. "Yeah. Good strange."

"The best," Luke answered in a voice rough with emotion.

While Beth finished getting dinner on the table, the men gathered in the living room and talked of sheep and fishing, baseball and oil prices. Soon they were wondering aloud if the west end of the county would get enough money for road maintenance this year, or if the Meeker area would once again get the bulk of the available county funds.

Ryan stuck his head into the kitchen. "Can we do it now, Mom?"

"You don't want to wait until after dinner?"

He grinned. "No."

She grinned back. "Okay, go ahead."

Ryan dashed down the hall to the bedroom and was back with the gifts before she had her hands dried.

This time it was Mr. Bower's reaction that brought a lump to Beth's throat.

"You...for me?" The old man's hands shook as he accepted the lumpy package. "Why...why, I don't know what to say."

Embarrassed but obviously pleased and excited, Ryan merely shrugged. "Hope you like it."

Mr. Bower held the package in his hands and turned it over and over, a smile lighting his face. "Kinda heavy."

"Well, hell, Ned," Leon said. "Don't keep us in suspense. Open it."

Mr. Bower worked his mouth. He licked his lips. Then he grinned again and ripped the green foiled paper away to find the chunk of wood within. "Ooo-wee, look at that. Why, why, ain't that something?"

"I found it out at the ranch. You like it?" Ryan asked.

"Like it? Well, of course I like it. You couldn'ta got me anything better."

"What are you gonna make with it?" Zach asked.

"Make? Hell, I don't make things, I just let 'em loose, don't you know."

"What do you think's in there?" Ryan asked.

Mr. Bower held the gnarled length of wood out, turned it, turned it again. With an almost reverent caress he said, "I do believe there might be a cougar in there."

"If anybody can find him," Ryan said, "you can."

When Mr. Bower looked up, his old eyes were glassy with emotion. "Thank you, young man. Thank you very much."

A moment later the others started reading their cards and unwrapping their gifts, exclaiming with pleasure over the things Ryan had chosen for them.

Afterward, Beth returned to the kitchen. Luke joined her a moment later. Memories of their date the night before swamped her, and suddenly Beth was embarrassed.

But last night wasn't what Luke had on his mind. "It was really nice of you to include Mr. Bower today. I know he gets lonesome."

Beth shook her head. "It was my idea to invite him, but the rest was Ryan's. He really likes him."

"When you raise kids, lady, you do damn fine work. Ryan is, well... There's not a thing about him I would change." *Except his address,* Luke thought. "In case I haven't said it lately, thank you."

She looked up slowly to find a haunted look in Luke's eyes that brought an ache to her chest. "For what?"

"For having him. For loving him. For letting me know him."

When Margaret saw the cars parked in front of Leon's house she nearly changed her mind about stopping. But she was afraid if she didn't go in there now and face him, tell him what she'd done, she might never find the courage to do it. Besides, what she had done had affected the lives of the others inside that house, too. They had a right to know.

In the end, it was her mother's smirk that motivated

her. "I told you you couldn't do it, dear," Rose said from the passenger seat. "But since you went to the trouble to finally put on some clothes and leave the house, we could eat dinner out for a change. The Cowboy Corral always has good specials on Sunday nights."

Margaret pulled up to the curb behind Luke's Lincoln and slapped the gearshift of her mother's Plymouth into Park. "We're here, and we're going in."

"I'm sure I have no such intention. Just tell me when you want me to pick you up."

"Oh, no." Margaret pulled the keys from the ignition and dropped them into her purse. "You're going in with me. You're going to hear what I say, you're going to *listen* in front of witnesses so you won't be able to twist my words later."

"You," Rose said with a dour look, "are making a big mistake."

Margaret took a deep breath for courage, grabbed her purse and swung open the car door. "It can't possibly be any bigger a mistake than the hundreds I've already made."

Sheer bravado carried her up the sidewalk and onto the porch. She knocked, and Beth answered.

"Mother! Grandma!" Shock held Beth immobile. Her mother had not set foot in the house since coming to town, nor had she made any attempt to speak to Leon after that one disastrous visit at the hospital.

And Grandma! What did she think she was doing here? If she'd come to cause more trouble...

"May we come in, Beth? I have some things I need to say. To all of you."

Beth cut her gaze to Rose, then back. "What's she doing here?"

"I want her to hear what I have to say, so she can't... I just want everything out in the open. Once and for all."

Beth glanced over her shoulder. Dinner was over and the men had migrated back to the living room. They were all watching her and her mother. All but Mr. Bower. He sat slumped in the corner of the sofa, his head lolled back, snoring softly.

Leon rose slowly from his chair and came to Beth's side. He stared at his wife with blank, lifeless eyes. "Margaret."

Margaret swallowed. "Leon. May I come in?"

"Why?"

Margaret jerked as if he'd slapped her. Then she straightened her chin and met his gaze. "I've brought you a Father's Day gift."

"I don't want anything from you."

"Not even the truth?"

Leon blinked. "What truth is that?"

"The real truth, Leon. It's all I have left to give you. Afterward, I'll...I'll leave you alone."

After a pause, he made a gesture over his shoulder. "We've got company." He pointed at Rose. "And that woman is not welcome under my roof."

Rose arched a penciled eyebrow. "Believe me, Leon, the feeling is mutual."

"Mother, shut up."

Rose gaped. So did Beth and Leon. To their knowledge, Margaret had never, *never* crossed her mother.

Leon stepped back from the door. "Come in. This could get interesting."

With one clenched fist slung through the handle of her purse, Margaret pressed the purse flat against her abdomen with the other hand and stepped past her daughter, past her husband whom she hadn't been this close to in sixteen years, and into the house she hadn't been inside in the same length of time.

"Hi, Gran, Grandma Rose," Ryan said.

Luke rose stiffly from the kitchen chair he'd brought into the living room. His hard gaze focused on Rose. "I think I'll head on home."

"Wait, Luke," Margaret said. "Please? You need to hear what I've come to say. All of you do," she added with a glance around the room.

In the corner Mr. Bower still slept. No one paid him any mind. Had he been awake, someone would undoubtedly have been forced to ask him to leave. After all, whatever Margaret had to say was surely family business. But since he slept, no one bothered to send him home.

After an awkward shuffling to find seats for everyone, Margaret ended up on a kitchen chair Ryan carried in for her.

Rose perched on the opposite end of the couch from Mr. Bower and shot him a look of disgust. Then she turned her gaze on Margaret. "Well, this was your idea. Do you still think you can do it?"

Margaret licked her lips. Ignoring her mother's gibe, she took a deep breath. "I assume all of you have learned by now about the lies Mother told that kept Beth and me from coming home all those years ago. For the record, she told me Leon was seeing another woman, and that Luke had married Carol Thompson. Mother can be...very persuasive. We believed her. Maybe I believed her because it helped justify what I'd done. You see, when Beth and I left on that vacation, even before Mother told her lies, I..." Margaret paused, gathering what courage she could find. "I never intended either of us to come home."

Except for an occasional quiet snore from Mr. Bower, the silence in the room was absolute and heavy with shock. Outside, birds chattered on their way to their nests for the night as the sun went down. Somewhere down the street a car door slammed, a child laughed.

Beth gaped at her mother, too stunned to respond.

Her father looked...tortured. "Why, Meg? For God's sake, why? I may not have been the best husband, but were things really that bad?"

Margaret shook her head slowly and closed her eyes a moment. When she looked at her husband again, it was through tears. "Only in my mind, Leon, and only because I was such a coward. God, this is hard."

"Mother?" Beth asked, still stunned. "Are you saying you *meant* to take me away and never bring me home?"

A strange calmness, shock, maybe, settled over Margaret. "Yes. That's what I'm saying. My mother got pregnant with me and had to marry my father. Because of that, she always felt trapped. In the marriage, in Rangely. Then it happened again, with me. I got pregnant with you, honey, and your father and I had to get married. When you were born..."

"When you were born, Beth," Rose said fiercely, "I vowed you would not become the third-generation female in this family to get stuck in a loveless marriage in this pitiful town. And I saw to it.''

"Yes, Mother,'' Margaret said sadly. "You saw to everything. You saw to it that no matter how much I loved Leon, no matter how happy we were, you kept reminding me that I *wasn't* happy. That I was trapped. That my life was over. Eventually you saw to it that I believed you. When Beth grew up, you saw how close she and Luke were getting, and you convinced me she deserved better. You convinced me it was nothing more than puppy love and teenage hormones.''

Margaret closed her eyes and raised her face to the ceiling. "God, what a fool I was to ever listen to you.'' She lowered her face and looked at Beth, then Leon, agony and shame pouring from her eyes. "But I did listen to her. I let her convince me she was right, that Beth needed a chance to get out in the world and have more choices than she would have here. I didn't want to go, didn't want to leave you or separate Beth and Luke, but I managed to convince myself it was best for Beth. So I deliberately turned myself into a shrew. I whined, I picked fights, I accused you of things. I manufactured anger, and used that to get Beth in the car that day and drive away, knowing full well I had no intention of ever coming back.

"But when I learned she was carrying Luke's child, I realized that not only was I too late in getting her away, I was wrong to have even thought about it in the first place. I decided right then that we were coming home. So I called Mother, and…and that's when she told us…well, you know the rest. Because of Mother and me, Ryan and Luke missed out on being father and son all these years. Ryan was cheated out of a family, Beth was cheated. Leon was cheated. So was Luke. I don't expect any of you to forgive me. I don't think I'll ever be able to forgive myself. I just thought you deserved to know."

"Cheated," Rose scoffed. "Who was cheated? Beth and Ryan have a wonderful life in Kansas City. She has a good career, he has the best schools, the three of you live in a beautiful home. And the third generation of women in this family did not get trapped in a stupid marriage, in a stupid little town."

Another taut silence stretched across the room. A moment later it was broken by the most unlikely source.

"My, my, Rosie," Mr. Bower said, startling everyone. "What a bunch of altruistic hogwash. You weren't trying to save anybody from anything, and you know it. Why don't you just come out and admit it? If little Bethany had fallen for anyone but a Ryan, you probably wouldn't have batted an eye."

"You senile old man, you don't know what you're talking about. Go back to sleep."

"Ha!" Mr. Bower sat forward on the couch and leaned toward her. "I know exactly what I'm talking about. I'm talking about Bill Ryan."

Rose paled with shock.

Zach narrowed his eyes. "What's my cousin have to do with anything?"

Mr. Bower rolled his eyes. "Guess none of you youngsters would know, but that summer Bill Ryan came to stay with you and your folks, Zach, Rose here did everything but stand on her head to get his attention. Heckfire, she probably *did* stand on her head. Probably showed her knickers while she was at it, too.''

It was a wonder *The Rangely Times* didn't fly off the coffee table and plaster itself across Rose's face, so sharply did she suck in air. "Ned Bower! How dare you! You know you can't remember what you ate for breakfast this morning, much less what happened more than fifty years ago. Nobody's going to believe a word you say, you old fool.''

"Oh, I remember what I need to." Mr. Bower chuckled. "You were really something back in those days, Rosie, ol' girl. You must have been what, fifteen? And wild as a March hare." The old man eyed the rest of the room. "When Bill Ryan wouldn't pay her any mind, she took up with Harvey Shoemaker, tryin' to make Bill jealous. Backfired real good, though, 'cause ol' Bill didn't give a care what she did. By the end of that summer her daddy was holdin' a shotgun on poor Harvey, and the next thing we know, there's a wedding and a baby, not necessarily in that order, if you get my drift. And Bill Ryan was long gone without ever givin' ol' Rosie so much as the time of day.''

The old man's gaze fastened hard on Rose. "I always wondered what would have happened if poor Harvey hadn't gone and got himself killed in the wreck out on Highway 40. Wonder if he'da been able to keep you in line. Because of Bill, you've hated every Ryan who ever came along since, haven't you, Rosie? My guess is, you'da rather seen your own granddaughter in her grave than watch her marry up with a Ryan.''

Rose's gaze darted sharply around the room, furtive, desperate. "Whatever happened to me has nothing to do with anything. I was right to make Margaret get Beth out of town. If they hadn't left, Beth wouldn't have a fine home and a good job, and Luke would never have gone to medical school. Beth would instead be trapped out on that pitiful wasteland you Ryans call a ranch, probably swelled up with baby number ten by now. Why should she be trapped here the rest of her life just because of a foolish accident?" she cried with a wave toward Ryan.

Ryan turned stricken eyes on Luke, then Beth.

Luke leapt from his chair. "Old woman, don't you *ever* use that tone or that word in reference to my son again."

"Besides," Beth said calmly, "it's not true."

"What's not true?" Margaret asked, puzzled.

Beth gave Luke a soft smile.

"Beth, don't," he warned. "There's no point. Not now."

"There's a very important point," she argued quietly. "That point is, the word *accident* has nothing to do with Ryan's birth."

"What are you saying?" her father asked.

"I'm saying, Daddy, that Luke and I knew that Mother, if not you, too, would have fought tooth and nail to keep Luke and me from getting married that summer after we graduated from high school. Mother wanted me to go to college. Luke and I decided to take the matter out of your hands. We purposely tried to get me pregnant so no one could keep us from getting married. I didn't know it worked, that I was pregnant, until Mother and I were on vacation."

She looked to Luke, but Luke wasn't listening.

"Where's Ryan?" he said, tension making his voice harsh.

Beth glanced around. "He was here just a minute ago." But he wasn't there now. Alarmed, she searched the room again.

"He slipped out the back door," Mr. Bower offered, fingering the piece of piñon Ryan had given him. "'Bout thirty seconds ago." He shot Rose a glare of pure animosity. "A tad hard on a youngster, being called an accident. Proud of yourself, Rosie?"

Beth jumped up and took two steps toward the back door before Luke stopped her. "Let me. I'll find him." The look in his eyes was fierce. "Besides, I don't trust myself in the same room with your grandmother another minute." He turned blazing eyes on Rose. "You just can't stop destroying lives, can you?"

Luke spun and hit the back door at a dead run, calling his son's name. "Ryan? Ryan!"

The yard was dark and empty. The only answer to Luke's call was the click of the back gate as it swung shut, and running footsteps up the alley blocked from view by the six-foot wooden fence.

Luke leapt from the porch, dashed down the sidewalk and shoved open the gate. He was just in time to see a shadow dart across the street at the end of the alley. Ryan was headed for the park.

"Ryan, wait!"

But Ryan didn't wait.

Damn you, Rose Shoemaker. Damn you.

Luke sprinted the length of the alley and across the street to the park. "Ryan!" The giant shadows of trees swallowed him. He paused, frantically scanning the darkness for movement, for sound, for some sign of his son.

"I'm here," Ryan said quietly from the shadows of a big elm. If he hadn't spoken, Luke would have run right past without seeing him.

Luke stepped into the shadows and found Ryan sitting in the damp grass with his arms locked around his raised knees. Luke lowered himself to the grass a few feet away, not wanting to crowd the boy. He felt cool dew seep into the seat of his jeans.

"Pretty lousy situation, huh?" Luke offered.

Ryan grunted. "You could say that," came his sarcastic reply.

Luke closed his eyes and prayed for guidance. What could he say to ease the hurt inflicted by a bitter old woman? He stared at the stars overhead, but no answer came. "You've got a right to be upset. We all do. But, son, try not to take anything your grandmother Rose says personally. She has no concept of other people's feelings. I'm not convinced she even has any feelings herself. I don't think she meant to hurt you."

"She didn't think calling me an accident would hurt?"

"I don't think she thought at all. Your gran, well, I think Margaret's going to have it worse than anybody, because she knows she hurt people, and I think she's honestly sorry for it. She saw what getting pregnant too young did to her mother, saw what she thought it was doing to her. She didn't want that for your mom. She knows now that there are better ways to deal with things than just running away. Besides, it didn't work, anyway. I'd already gotten your mother pregnant by then.''

"So what I'm supposed to learn from all this is to keep my pecker in my pants, right?'' Ryan asked.

Luke chuckled. "Son, men have been ignoring that advice since before they had pants to keep their peckers in. But you might want to keep in mind how many people you can hurt with a careless act.''

"Was I a careless act?''

The question sent a tremor of pain rattling through Luke's chest. No child should ever have to ask such a question. But his child did. Luke took a deep breath to steady his voice. "I guess you didn't stick around long enough to hear what your mother had to say about that.''

Ryan pulled a handful of wet grass loose from the earth and started tossing it away one blade at a time.

"You were not an accident, Ryan.''

"Of course I was. But hey, it's no big deal. Happens all the time. You and Mom got carried away, and nine months later, there I was, the little accident, the little bastard.''

Luke ached with the need to reach out to his son, but the way Ryan hunched his shoulders and kept himself turned partially away held him back. God, what a mess.

"Technically, yes, you're a bastard,'' Luke said, hating the word so much it made his throat burn just saying it, "because your mother and I never married. But you were never an accident, Ryan. Never. Your mother and I loved each other very much. Maybe we weren't too smart about it, but your birth was no accident.''

Ryan cocked his head and looked at Luke out of the corner of his eye. "How come?"

Luke gave a half smile. "We wanted to get married. Your mom was convinced that her mother and grandmother were going to try to force her to go away to college. We figured... Damn, this is a heck of a thing to admit to a teenager, and don't get the idea in your head that what we did was the right way to solve our particular problem, but we figured if she got pregnant, they'd have to let us get married. You know better than anybody that things didn't work out like we planned. But we have you, and you were planned. Don't ever forget that, Ryan. You were planned, you were wanted. And not just as an excuse for us to get married. We wanted a big family, lots of kids. You were to be the first."

Ryan made no response. They sat quietly for a while, listening to the crickets singing in the dew.

"So what happens now?" Ryan finally asked. "Are you and Mom... What I mean is...are you two gonna get back together?"

Ah, yes. The question of the century. "What does your mother say?"

"Nothing. That's why I'm asking you."

"The only answer I have is, I don't know. We're taking things one step at a time."

Ryan looked up with wide, questioning eyes. "Do you love her?"

This was the question that, until last night, Luke had been avoiding since the day Beth had come back to town. The answer was easy now.

Even five minutes before he saw her that day at the hospital, he would have sworn there was no way he had any tender feelings left for Beth Martin. No way in hell.

All it had taken was one look to know he'd been wrong.

The answer to Ryan's question came at Luke from all sides, from his heart, his head, his very soul. "Yes," he said softly. "I love her more than ever."

Chapter Fourteen

Leon came to the clinic for his checkup Monday, and Luke was pleased to be able to give him a clean bill of health. Less than a month earlier, Luke hadn't been sure Leon would ever walk out of the hospital.

"Thanks, Luke," Leon said sincerely.

"Don't thank me, Leon. You did most of the work. Just don't get sick again."

"I'll do my best. 'Course, you could sure help keep me in good spirits if you'd do something about keeping a certain young woman and her son in town for about the next thirty years or so."

Luke gave him a wry grin. "I'm working on it."

"Hmmph. Doesn't look like you're doing much good. She's sitting out there in that office right now looking like somebody just came along with a pair of pliers and pulled all her teeth."

Luke sighed. "I know. She's still upset about last night, and I can't say I blame her. Has she said anything to you about her mother?"

Leon's expression closed off. "We haven't talked about it."

"I imagine she needs a little time with it. I imagine you both do. I don't want to rush her."

"Hmmph. You rush her any less, you'll be going backward, boy. If you let her leave town again, you're not half the man I think you are."

"Don't worry, Leon. I don't have any intention of letting her leave just yet."

Telling Leon not to worry was easy enough, but Luke had trouble taking his own advice. It should have been impossible for Beth to avoid him, when they worked in the same clinic together each day, but somehow she managed it. She never let him catch her alone, and she withdrew further from him each day. By Wednesday the sadness in her eyes had him more than worried, more than scared. It had him terrified. She was slipping away from him, sure and fast.

With determination, he clamped down on his fear and stopped her in the hall as she was leaving Wednesday evening. "How are you doing?" he asked quietly.

She shrugged and gave him a halfhearted smile. "Okay."

The bleakness in her eyes chilled him, but he forced a smile. "I'm not on call tomorrow night. How about letting me take you and Ryan to dinner and a movie in Vernal? Just the three of us. What do you say?"

Beth rubbed at the persistent ache in her right temple. She knew she wasn't being fair to Luke, that he deserved an explanation for the way she'd been avoiding him. In truth, she wasn't sure exactly why she'd been holding him at arm's length since Sunday night. She just had these vague fears running around inside her head. She needed to deal with them, sort them out and conquer them, not put them on Luke's shoulders.

"Beth?"

"Sorry, I was thinking. Why don't you and Ryan go without me? I really need to stay by the phone."

"Why? What's wrong?"

"I...I went to Grandma's yesterday to talk to Mother." She raised her gaze to his. The devastation there made his arms ache to hold her.

"She's gone, Luke. Mother packed her clothes Sunday night after leaving Dad's, got in her rental car and took off without a word to anyone."

Luke gave her a hard smile. "Sounds familiar to me. She's pretty good at that."

At Beth's stricken look, he lowered his gaze and shook his head. His feelings for Margaret's part in his sixteen-year separation from Beth and Ryan were his problem. The woman was, after all, Beth's mother. "I'm sorry. That's history, I know. This time I can't really blame her for leaving. She probably needed some time alone after that scene Sunday night. She probably just wanted to go home."

"But she didn't go home. At least, if she did, she's not answering the phone and hasn't even rewound the message tape. I checked this morning, and all the old messages are still there. I'm worried, Luke."

"Babe." He squeezed her shoulders gently, stung

that she'd been so worried and hadn't let him know. "Why didn't you tell me?"

"I didn't want to bother you with my problems. You've handled enough garbage from my family as it is."

Luke stiffened and dropped his hands from her shoulders. After all he and Beth had shared, in the distant past, and especially last Saturday night in each other's arms, her words hurt. Like falling down a tunnel through time, his old reaction to pain caused by Beth Martin reared its head. The only way he'd been able to deal with the pain before had been to substitute anger in its place. He did so now unconsciously.

"Well, thanks," he snapped. "I appreciate the hell out of being kept out of your business. What am I, some stranger all of a sudden?"

"I didn't mean it like that," she said quickly.

Luke clenched his jaw and turned away. "Never mind. I'll give Ryan a call and see if he wants to go tomorrow night."

All the next day and night, even while enjoying the time he spent with his son, Luke kicked himself for letting Beth off the hook so easily. Kicked himself, and cussed her. Damn her, she was shutting him out as if he was no more important than a pesky cold draft swirling around her feet. How could she do that after what they'd shared the previous week? How could she give herself to him so sweetly, so completely, tell him she loved him, then turn around and practically cut him out of her life?

Why not? a voice in the back of his mind mocked. *She did it before, didn't she?*

One part of Luke said to hell with her. If she hadn't believed in him enough sixteen years ago to call and ask him for the truth... Did he really want a woman who trusted him so little?

Yet when the woman was Beth, the answer rang forcefully in his mind. Yes. He wanted her. In his life, in his bed. She was already in his blood, his heart, his mind. He wanted a life, a future, with her and their son. He wanted to ask her to give him more children. He wanted her to need him the way he needed her, the way he needed air to breathe.

As he'd told her last week, though, she obviously didn't need him. Funny, but the thought hurt more now than it had just a few days ago. Because now, again, he felt closer to her than anyone in the world. Because now they'd made love. Because now, when she was hurt and confused, instead of sharing her feelings with him, she closed him out to deal with them on her own.

But Beth wasn't dealing with her feelings, she was hiding from them. Or trying to. Pain, disillusionment, anger, confusion. Worry, guilt and fear. They tumbled around inside her and took turns strangling her.

The pain was maybe a little for herself, but mostly for her father. It was one thing for him to know his wife had believed her mother's lies about him, quite another to learn the only woman he'd ever loved, whom he thought loved him, had, after nearly nineteen years of marriage, coolly, deliberately, taken their daughter and left him without a word.

Most of the other feelings battling inside Beth were over her mother. Disillusionment. Anger, certainly.

The betrayed teenager inside her demanded anger. But the parent in her understood to what lengths a mother might go to give her child what she thought best, and that tempered her anger. The tempering brought confusion. Her mother had deliberately plotted to keep her away from Luke, and from her father. How could Beth so easily forgive such deceit?

Yet how could she not? The alternative, to turn her back on her own mother, was unthinkable. Her mother had been the mainstay of Beth's life, the one stable influence when her world had fallen apart. Margaret might have started the rock slide that had nearly buried Beth, but she'd also done her best to see her through the rough times.

"Oh, Mother, what are we going to do? Where are you? I need to see you."

But Thursday night passed with no word from Margaret Martin, no trace of her to be found.

Friday was Beth's last day at the clinic, and it was all she could do to go through the motions of the daily routine. What was she going to do after the reunion tomorrow night? Should she stay or should she go? What was best for Ryan—a life with both his parents? Or would he rather go home to Kansas City?

And even if they stayed in Rangely permanently, the three of them might never be a real family. Luke said he loved her, but he'd never asked her to stay. Not really. He'd said he wanted a life with her and Ryan, but it would be presumptuous in the extreme for her to think Luke wanted to marry her.

Then there was her mother to consider. Should

Beth stay in town and wait to hear from her or go home and look for her from there?

Beth put the last of the files away and turned to find Dr. O'Grady at the window that opened into the waiting room. "No more patients today, Doctor. Mrs. Murphy was the last one."

"And a fine one she was, too."

Beth laughed at the look of angelic innocence beaming from his face. Everyone in town knew that the widow Murphy had been hot after Dr. Carlos O'Grady for two years. The woman had been in twice this week with a vague ache here, a weakness there. Beth suspected the weakness was around the woman's heart, but she managed to lead Carlos on a merry chase, even while she chased him.

"I guess this is it for you, huh?" he asked Beth.

"Yep. My last day. I'm on my way out now."

"Well, if you change your mind and decide to stay, you've got my recommendation for the job."

If she stayed. If she moved back to Rangely and worked full-time at the clinic. With Luke. Luke, who hadn't asked her to stay. "Thank you, Carlos, I appreciate that. Maybe I'll see you around town this weekend."

They said goodbye, and Beth picked up her purse and turned to go. Luke stood in the doorway, blocking her exit. At the sight of him, she tensed.

Carlos looked from one to the other, noted the muscle bunching in Luke's jaw, and backed away. "I'm outa here. See you two later." His footsteps faded down the hall, leaving only the faint hum of fluorescent lights to fill the silence.

"He's right, you know," Luke said.

"About what?"

"If you wanted the job permanently, I'm sure you could get it."

Beth looked down and ran her thumbnail along the decorative groove in the clasp on her purse.

"Are you even thinking about staying?" he demanded. "Or are your bags packed?"

Beth tossed her head up. "I never said I'd stay. You never asked me to."

He looked away a moment, then, with a sharp nod, met her gaze. "All right, I'm asking. Will you stay?"

She should have kept her mouth shut. Now what was she supposed to say? What, exactly, was he asking? That she stay in town so he could see Ryan whenever he wanted? Or was he asking for something else entirely, something personal?

As if he'd read her mind, he said, "You know what I'm asking, Beth, you know how I feel about you. I want you and Ryan and me to be a family, the way we should have been all these years."

Pain and uncertainty constricted her throat. "After all that's happened, everything my mother and grandmother have done, all the strife and tension pulling us this way and that, would we even have a chance at a normal life?"

The muscle in his jaw bunched again. "You ask that like you've already decided we can't make it work. Is that really what you think?"

"I don't know what to think," she cried, the pressure of the past week tying her nerves in knots.

"When will you know?" he demanded.

"Don't push me on this, Luke."

"Don't push?" he cried. "How can I not push?

You're going to let them do it again, aren't you? You're going to let them destroy us. Sixteen years ago you listened to your mother and your grandmother, let them manipulate you right out of my life, let them convince you to deny me my son. Now here you are, doing it again.''

''I am not! I won't have Ryan tearing himself apart trying to decide where his loyalties lie. I'm trying to think what would be best for him.''

''Yeah, right. Like your mother thought about what was best for you. That's bull, and you know it.''

She gripped her purse more tightly until the metal clasp cut into her palm. ''Why is it bull?''

Luke's jaw hardened. His eyes narrowed to angry slits. ''All this talk about family strife and not wanting Ryan exposed to it. Hell, it's just another excuse to run out on me. If you knew for sure your mother was in Kansas City, you'd grab Ryan and be back there so fast my stomach turns over just thinking about it.''

Calm. She had to stay calm. She didn't want to argue with him. ''Luke, you're not being fair. No matter what she's done, she's still my mother. She needs me.''

''Well, now, that has a familiar ring to it. When she wanted to get out of town for a few days all those years ago, she needed you then, too, didn't she? Guess that tells me where I stand, doesn't it?''

''Dammit, Luke—''

''Don't 'dammit Luke' me. *I* need you. I needed you sixteen years ago, too, but you just had to go on that vacation. 'Mother needs me,' you said.''

''Haven't I paid long enough for that?' she cried.

"Haven't *I*? I paid, too, Beth. I paid for sixteen years for something I had no control over. I'm still paying. I spilled my guts to you the other night in my bed. My guts, and a good deal more. But do you give a damn how much I love you? No, not you. All you wanted me for was a little test drive for the ol' libido. Well, babe, you can rest easy on that score. Feel free to use me as a reference anytime. I can testify to exactly how hot you can burn."

To hell with staying calm. The anger coursing through her veins felt good, healing. She nursed it along, let it override the pain of his words. With narrowed eyes and clenched fists she glared at him. "How dare you?"

"Oh, I dare. The same way you dare to pop back into my life after all this time. Give me a taste of heaven, then walk out on me again. God, I was a fool to ever think I stood a chance with you, then or now. Go on, dammit. Do it again. Take my son and run on back to Kansas City, where you don't have to deal with meddling relatives or a man who expects the one thing you can't give—a little loyalty. Have a nice life, Bethany. I intend to do the same. I'll be in touch about Ryan coming back whenever he can."

Slivers of ice trailed down Beth's spine as she watched Luke turn away. She called his name, but he kept walking. Damn him! He couldn't do this to her! He wasn't even giving her a chance. She didn't know whether to swear, cry or scream.

Once she made it to the privacy of her bedroom, the only thing Beth managed to choke back was the scream, but the sound she made when she buried her face in her pillow came mighty close to one. The swearing and the tears followed quickly.

Damn Luke Ryan. She hadn't cried as much in years as she had since coming back to Rangely. Did he expect her to just ignore that her mother was missing, that her father hadn't said two words to anyone all week, that her son was being pulled apart, loving them all and not understanding why they had to hurt each other?

All she needed was a little time to sort things out in her mind, but Luke wasn't willing to wait.

He waited sixteen years, Beth.

She cried harder.

By midafternoon Saturday, the day of the class reunion, there was still no word of Margaret. Leon left to take Ryan to the ranch for the weekend while Beth stayed near the phone. Just in case.

She paced from the kitchen table through the living room to the front door and back. Again and again. Table, living room, door. Door, living room, table. She tried to concentrate on where her mother might have gone, but all she could seem to think about was Luke.

Have a nice life.

She squeezed her eyes shut. How the hell was she supposed to have any kind of life while her family was tearing itself apart? How was she supposed to have a life without Luke?

As angry as she still was at his high-handed attitude, she could plainly see his side of the situation. And she knew that, no matter what, she still loved him.

And he expected her to walk away. Did he have so little faith in her?

Yes, he obviously did. With reason, too, if she was honest. She'd had even less faith in him all those years ago, to think he could possibly have married Carol. God, what a fool she'd been. A young, terrified, pregnant, *stupid* fool.

In a whirl of confusion, pain and self-disgust, she threw herself down on the couch and flung an arm across her eyes. To stem the flow of emotions she tried to turn her mind to practical matters. What was she going to do about tonight's reunion? Luke certainly wasn't about to take her now.

Out on the street a car slowed down and stopped somewhere nearby.

Dammit, Luke, I didn't mean to push you away.

In the kitchen the refrigerator cycled off, leaving the only man-made sound in the house the lonely ticking of the old windup alarm clock on her father's nightstand. Outside, a car door slammed. Footsteps scraped on the sidewalk. Her father must be back from the ranch already.

The hollow thump of feet on the wooden porch sounded dull to Beth's ears. A shadow blocked the light coming through the storm door. She kept her arm across her eyes, not ready to face anyone just yet.

The door swung open. "Hello, Beth."

"Mother!" Beth sprang from the couch. She stood frozen a moment, unsure what to do. At the uncertainty on her mother's face, Beth launched herself across the room and hugged her. "Are you all right? Where have you been? We've been so worried."

Margaret returned the hug, then stood back. Tears

glinted in her eyes, and her lips trembled. "I was afraid," she said haltingly, "you wouldn't want to see me."

"Don't be silly. Come. Sit down and tell me where you've been. Did you go home?"

With a sad smile, Margaret lowered herself to the couch. "Home? Where is that? We've called Missouri home for so long, but this place…" She gazed around the room, pausing on one familiar piece after another.

"I know what you mean," Beth said slowly, following her mother's gaze around the room. "In some ways, it's like we never left."

"I was headed back to Kansas City when I left here," Margaret said with a sniff. "I only got as far as Rifle. I've been in a motel there since Sunday night. I kept telling myself to just get on the interstate for Grand Junction and take the next plane out. But I couldn't do it. Something here didn't feel…finished."

Margaret blinked the faraway glaze from her eyes. "We never should have gone away all those years ago." She bowed her head. "I never should have taken you from here. But Beth," she said, raising her head and meeting Beth's gaze, "whatever your grandmother and I have done, however much you may hate us, don't let that interfere with whatever you and Luke might still feel for each other."

"I…I don't hate you, Mother."

Margaret swallowed. "I hope you mean that. But you didn't answer me about Luke."

This time it was Beth who hung her head. "There's nothing to say."

"Isn't there? What about the fact that you still love him, that despite what you thought he did to you, you never stopped?"

Beth looked up. "Why do you say that?"

"Because I'm your mother, and I know you. Then, too, we're a lot alike in many ways. We don't love easily or lightly, you and I. Don't repeat my mistakes, Beth. Don't let go of Luke, not for anything. Love is too important, too precious."

"Strange advice, coming from you."

"Leon!"

"Daddy!" Beth hadn't heard him come in the back way. His voice from the kitchen doorway nearly stopped her heart. "You scared the daylights out of me."

But he didn't look at Beth. His stare centered directly on Margaret. "So. You gonna fish, or cut bait?"

Margaret paled. "What...what do you mean?"

"I *mean*, are you and I going to talk, really talk, or are you going to run out on me again?"

Beth's throat went dry. She looked from one parent to the other, saw how intently their gazes locked. She could practically feel the electric tension humming between them. Her father was hurt and angry and trying not to show it. Her mother was hopeful and scared and showing it plainly.

They didn't need her presence. This was private. "I, uh, I'll be back later. You two need to talk." She grabbed her purse and car keys and lit straight for the front door.

Once in her car, Beth drove to the stop sign where Stanolind hit Main. Her first thought was to turn east and drive out to the ranch and spend some time with Ryan, but she discarded the idea. Luke was all too likely to be there. He'd just worked his twelve straight days; today was the first of his nine-days-off stretch. She knew she had to talk with him, *wanted* to talk with him, but not in front of Ryan and the rest of Luke's family.

Behind her, a car horn honked. Beth jerked, wondering how long she had been sitting there. She put her foot on the gas and turned left. In seconds she was past the west edge of town, heading nowhere.

Chapter Fifteen

The line of people waiting their turn at the buffet table snaked around the edge of the echoing auditorium and inched slowly forward. Large round tables, with chairs for eight at each, took up the center of the room. The turnout for the class reunion had everyone excited.

Voices surged, shouted and laughed. Flashbulbs blinded. Wallets whipped out of purses and pockets on command and flipped open to pictures of children, houses, pets, boats. Up close, the smell of ink on slick paper in fifteen- and sixteen-year-old high school annuals overpowered the aroma of barbecue. At least three video cameras captured hugs, smiles and dirty jokes.

Luke had arrived late and was stuck near the end of the food line. By the time he finally reached his turn at the buffet some thirty minutes later, he was wishing wholeheartedly that the turnout hadn't been quite so good. It seemed every person in the room had asked him at least once why Beth wasn't with him. Small towns definitely had their disadvantages when a man didn't want to answer questions.

With his paper plate piled high with more food than he could possibly eat, Luke paused before taking a chair next to Fran and Tom Woodward. He scanned the room yet again, searching for a dark, glossy head, a pair of laughing gray-green eyes, a particular soft smile. Maybe a yellow-gold sundress held up by skinny straps.

As on the other dozen or so searches he'd made since his arrival, he found no sign of Beth. And for the dozenth time he told himself to stop looking. She wasn't coming.

And why should she, after the way he'd treated her yesterday? He took his seat. The voices of his table-mates buzzed around him as they laughed and talked over old times. Luke hoped he made the appropriate noises, but his mind was elsewhere. What a bastard he'd been, losing his cool with Beth like some kid who'd had his favorite toy snatched away. She'd been hurt and confused, and he'd acted like a damn bear, pushing her, slinging accusations like the jerk he was.

He had to apologize. That was all there was to it. And he had to do it soon, or she'd be gone. Suddenly he stiffened, his gaze locked on his plate of half-eaten food. Good God. *What if she's already gone?*

No! She couldn't be. She wouldn't just run out without a word. She wouldn't do it, no matter that he'd accused her of planning that very thing. No matter that he'd practically taunted her into doing it. She wouldn't.

On an oath, Luke shoved back his chair.

"Hey, man, what gives?" Tom asked.

"I just remembered a call I have to make." With no further explanation, Luke rushed to the hall and the nearest pay phone. His hands shook while he dialed Leon's number and listened to the phone ring. And ring, and ring. And ring.

"Son of a bitch." He slammed the phone down and dialed the ranch. On the third ring his dad answered.

"Is Ryan still there?"

"Well, hello to you, too. I thought you were at your class reunion."

"Just answer me, Dad. Is Ryan still there?"

"Of course he is."

Luke's knees went weak with relief. She wasn't gone. She wouldn't leave without Ryan.

"We're just gettin' ready to eat supper. You wanna talk to him?"

It took Luke three tries to get his voice to work. "No, that's okay. Just…tell him I'll see him tomorrow." Without waiting for a reply, Luke hung up. For a moment he rested his forehead against the receiver and willed his hands to stop shaking. She hadn't left yet. She hadn't left.

Voices at the end of the hall had him straightening away from the phone.

"Luke," Carol called. She turned to the three women with her. "I'll catch up in a minute. I need to talk to Luke."

The others waved at him and rejoined the crowd

beyond the big double doors. Carol stopped beside him. "Where's Beth? I've been looking for her all evening."

Luke sighed. "You have to be the only person here who hasn't already asked me that."

She raised a brow. "And what are you telling them?"

He shrugged. "That she'll probably be along later."

"And will she? What's going on, Luke? She was really looking forward to tonight. Why isn't she here? Why isn't she with you?"

Carol was too good a friend, to both him and Beth, for him to lie. With the thumb and forefinger of one hand he rubbed his eyes. "We had a...slight disagreement. I don't know where she is."

Carol folded her arms across her chest and glared at him. "I swear, I'm going to take the two of you down and sit on you, if that's what it takes to straighten you out. You guys have been separated for sixteen years. You've got no business fighting. You ought to be planning on just how fast you can get her stuff moved and when the wedding's going to be. You *have* asked her to marry you, haven't you?"

Her words hit him like a punch in the gut. He'd told Beth he wanted a life with her and Ryan. He'd said he wanted them to be a family. He'd told her he loved her, that he'd never stopped loving her in all their years apart. Could she really doubt that he wanted to marry her?

"Luke?"

Yes, she could doubt. With all her mother and grandmother had put her through, with all the trauma from all the lies, with all the years she had thought he'd betrayed her, Beth would have need of the words he'd unwittingly withheld. Damn, why hadn't he just come right out and asked her to marry him?

"You idiot," Carol snapped. "If you don't get out of here right this minute and go find her, I'm personally going to whack you upside the head."

"Go ahead," he said dryly. "I've already got it coming."

"Just go get her."

"I called the house. She's not there."

"Then maybe she's on her way here. I know she was planning on coming. We talked on the phone yesterday about what to wear."

"When yesterday?"

"I don't know. Early afternoon, I think."

Early afternoon. Before he'd told her off and walked away. But maybe Carol was right. Even if Beth was planning on leaving town, she would still want to see their old classmates again. Wouldn't she?

With a deep breath for patience, he decided to give her a little more time. If she didn't show up by the time dinner was over and the crowd left the college for the dance at the Chevron Rec Hall, he would go after her.

She didn't show up.

He went after her.

Margaret's rental car was parked in front of Leon's. So. She'd come back.

But the house was dark and no one answered the door. Where the hell could Beth be? He ran by his house and called the ranch again, but she hadn't been there.

Luke swore as he hung up the phone and headed for the rec hall. He was going to have some tall explaining to do to his dad tomorrow, for all his questioning tonight.

He thought briefly about staying home in case Beth came by, but discarded the idea. She knew where he'd planned to be tonight. If she went looking for him, which under the circumstances was damned unlikely, she would look at the dance.

Before heading to the rec hall west of town, Luke dragged Main a couple of times looking for her car. He didn't find it.

He checked his watch. It was eight forty-five. Where the hell could she be?

At nine-thirty Beth spotted Luke's Mark VII near the side door of the Chevron Rec Hall and pulled in behind it, purposely blocking him in. She didn't care how mad he was at her, he was going to listen.

When she stepped out of her car, country music blasted from the open doorway at the side of the building. With sweating palms she straightened her new calf-length denim skirt and shook out the layers of blended cotton ruffles down the arms of her new white blouse. She'd bought the clothes, as well as the Western boots she was wearing, this afternoon in Vernal.

She hadn't planned on driving that far when she'd headed west out of town. She'd driven out State Highway 64 through the oil fields, across the Green River, and ended up in Dinosaur where 64 ended at its junction with U.S. 40. The tiny town hadn't changed much over the years. There was nothing there to hold her interest. She'd gone west on 40, crossed the state line into Utah and ended up in Vernal, some fifty miles from Rangely.

By then it had been late afternoon, and she knew she would have to hurry to make it to the reunion. But that reminded her she had nothing she wanted to wear, and the night, if Luke would let it, would be a special one. She wanted to look her best.

So after a late lunch, she'd gone shopping. She hadn't intended to spend so much time—or money. When she'd driven back and reached the Chevron building, she'd known she had already missed the class dinner, and the dance had started. She'd rushed home and found her mother's car still parked out front, but the house was dark and empty. After looking for a note from her father and not finding one, Beth showered and changed clothes, then rushed back to the rec hall past the edge of town.

With another swipe of her palms down her skirt, she started for the door. She didn't have the slightest idea what she would say to Luke. As dry as her mouth was and the way her hands and knees were shaking, she'd be lucky to get two words out before she lapsed into gibberish.

As she cautiously approached the open door she barely heard the scrape of her new boots along the ground. She barely heard the loud music, the shouts, the laughter from inside the building. All she could hear was her own blood pounding in her ears.

Standing in the doorway, Beth scanned the room. It was decorated in the school colors. Streamers, banners and posters. Green and white forever. Go Panthers.

Dozens of folding chairs surrounded long tables. The lights were low, with colored spots glowing in the corners. People, her classmates from years ago, looking much the same as when she'd known them so well, sat or milled or danced, all smiling, laughing, having a good time.

The song changed from fast to slow, from loud and rowdy Hank Williams, Jr., to a Garth Brooks ballad. Then she saw Luke. Her breath caught in her throat and hung there. Her new boots seemed suddenly rooted in the open doorway. He stood facing her, leaning against the wall near the opposite doorway, talking to a man a full head shorter than he with a bald spot on the back of his head. Tom Woodward.

Luke rubbed a hand across his mouth and scanned the room. Beth waited, breath held, until he spotted her. In slow motion, as if with great effort, he lowered his hand to his side and straightened away from the wall. His eyes locked on hers and held her immobile. She stood frozen, like a butterfly pinned to a twig in a school science exhibit. His first step in her direction freed her.

They met at the front of the room along the edge of the dance floor, the musical vibration from the huge speakers making the floor tremble beneath them. Or maybe it was Beth's own shaking she was feeling.

They stopped mere inches from each other. She could feel his heat, in sharp contrast to the coolness from the open door behind her. The starch in his blue shirt smelled clean and mingled with the hint of tangy after-shave.

"Beth—"

She placed her fingers across his mouth. The way he closed his eyes and slowly inhaled sent her pulse pounding. Eyes still closed, he grasped her upper arms and whispered her name against her fingers.

A shudder of aching response traveled through her. When he looked at her, his eyes pulled her into his embrace. His encircling arms brought her close, closer, until her breasts met the muscled wall of his chest. It was a full minute before she realized they were swaying to the slow throb of the music.

"I love you," she said to him.

His eyes darkened at her admission.

"I'm sorry I shut you out. I didn't mean—"

"Shh." He brushed his nose against her cheek. "I'm sorry, too. I acted like a jerk. I love you. I don't want you to leave."

"I couldn't. I could never walk away from you again. Not ever."

As he buried his face in her hair, his arms closed more tightly around her back. "Let's get out of here."

For the fewer than ten minutes it took to get to his house, Luke kept one eye on the road, the other on Beth's headlights in his rearview mirror. She had come. She still loved him. Still wanted him.

Thank God.

His hands shook with nerves and eagerness while he stood beside his car in his garage a few minutes later and waited for her to park in his driveway. Before she could get out of the car, he went to her open window. "Do you want to put yours in the garage so your grandmother won't see it here?"

Her grin was slow and sultry. "Not unless it's going to embarrass you to have the whole neighborhood see it when they get up in the morning."

He yanked her car door open and reached for her wrist. "Come here."

She barely had time to grab her keys and purse before he pulled her from the car and into his arms. His aching need for her took the upper hand and he kissed her, hard and long and fiercely. When he tore his mouth free he was all but supporting her weight. Her eyes threatened to swallow him whole and burn him to cinders with their heat.

"We'll both be embarrassed if we don't get in the house right now," he warned, only half joking. "If you don't stop looking at me like that, we're going to end up rolling around naked in my front yard."

Her answering shiver shot fire straight to his loins. With a groan, he pulled her aside and slammed the car door shut, then led her in through the garage. At the door to the kitchen he pushed the button on the wall, and the garage door slid closed behind them.

When he shut the door from the kitchen to the garage, the kitchen was pitch-black. Instead of reaching for the light switch, he reached for Beth. Her arms came around his neck and clung so sweetly, the ache in his chest intensified.

"God, babe, I'm sorry I said all those things to you. I didn't mean them, not really. I felt you shutting me out and it hurt. I guess I was just trying to hurt you back."

"I know." She kissed his jaw, his chin. "I know I hurt you, and I'm sorry, too. I swear, Luke, I'll never give you cause to doubt me again."

"You didn't give me cause this time. I think this was just my own insecurities acting up. I was so scared you would leave me. Don't leave me, Beth."

"Never. Never."

He tasted tears on her cheeks. "Don't cry. Please don't cry." He covered her lips with his and with one arm around her shoulders, the other beneath her knees, carried her through the dark house to his bedroom, with nothing to guide him but habit and the soft sighs of the woman in his arms.

Luke laid her gently on the bed and followed her down. A sense of peace enveloped him, chasing away the urgency clawing in his gut. There was no hurry. She was his, and she was staying. They had the rest of their lives together.

With soft words and softer kisses, they slowly undressed each other. As if reading each other's mind, they purposely took their time, dragging the sensual disrobing out slowly, one touch, one article of clothing, one bared inch of skin at a time.

But the leisurely pace was impossible to maintain. With each touch, with each kiss, the fever built until Beth writhed beneath his weight. "Luke," she breathed.

"I'm here, babe. Right here." And he was. Pushing into her one exquisite inch at a time until they were joined, body, mind and soul.

Skin heated, breath rasped and mingled, rhythm pounded faster and faster, and the fever pitched higher and higher until together, Luke and Beth soared over the edge.

* * *

"I looked for you tonight. At the dinner, then afterward, when I drove by your house."

Beth searched his face in the dim glow of the streetlight outside on the corner. "I'm sorry I was late. I went for a drive and ended up in Vernal. I didn't mean to be gone so long."

He gave her a slow, deep kiss. "It was worth the wait. I love you."

She sighed and stretched against him. "I love you, too."

"Does that mean you'll marry me?"

"Yes!"

He grinned. "You don't want to think about it awhile, keep me dangling for a few days?"

Beth pursed her lips and shook her head. "I don't think we should wait."

"Good." He kissed her again, trailing a hand across her hip. "I want you again. Always. Years ago you were my strength. Now you're my weakness. I'll never get enough of you. I don't want to wait another day to finally make you mine."

"I've always been yours," she told him softly. "But you're right. We shouldn't wait."

He eyed her carefully, a crease lining his brow. "You say that like you have a specific reason for hurrying."

"Well...I don't know about you, but since we didn't use any protection just now, I'm sure I don't want to have to explain to my father that you got me pregnant *again.*"

Luke hooted with laughter and hugged her close. Then he sobered. "Would you mind? Getting pregnant, I mean."

The smile came from deep within her soul. "Not

for a minute. But I thought you wanted to wait. Last week you said—"

"Never mind last week. I don't want to wait. We've lost so many years already, let's not waste another minute."

"But I might not be pregnant yet, you know. I mean, there's only been this one time."

"Like I said," he told her as he leaned down, "let's not waste another minute."

The doorbell woke them at 12:22 the next afternoon. Luke swore. Beth nuzzled her nose into the hair on his chest.

The doorbell rang again.

When Luke made to rise, Beth came fully awake and looked up at him with a smile so tender it slammed into his chest and knocked the breath out of him. To hell with the doorbell, and to hell with whoever was ringing it. Luke had better things to do.

Her lips were warm and soft, sweet and drugging. Her arms held him in bed more surely than any chains could have.

The doorbell rang again.

"Damn." He dropped his head back against the pillow. "With timing like this, that has to be J.D. out there. He's probably wondering why I didn't show up at church. I'll get rid of him."

After another quick kiss, this one hard and fast, Luke ignored the rising heat in his loins and forced himself from the bed. He stepped into his jeans, zipped them and stumbled from the room.

The doorbell rang twice more before he could answer it. When he reached the door he flung it open. "Dammit to hell and back..."

His words ended in a strangled cough at the sight of Leon and Margaret Martin standing side by side on his front porch. He felt the blush start at his navel and race up his chest clear past his forehead.

Leon eyed Beth's car in the driveway, then, with pursed lips, gave Luke a cool once-over.

Luke fumbled to fasten the brass button on his fly. Margaret blushed.

Leon's eyes narrowed. "I assume Beth is here?"

"Uh..."

"Daddy? Mother?"

Luke's breath left him in a loud whoosh. Heaven help him. Caught like a couple of overeager teenagers by her parents. He turned to offer Beth a quiet apology, only to choke on the words. Good God. She'd come to the door wearing nothing but the wrinkled shirt he'd had on last night. The tail hung almost to her knees, but the sides of the shirt were cut high enough to threaten exposure of much more intimate flesh.

Her hair was mussed and looked as if a man had just run his fingers through it, which was the unvarnished truth. Her lips were puffy and moist, and the glow in her eyes was unmistakably that of a woman aroused.

"I think," Leon said from the door, "you'd better invite us in, son."

And I think, Luke decided as he stepped back and ushered the Martins inside, *that I'm dead meat.*

Aside from the inherent embarrassment—and humor, Beth admitted with a glance at Luke's blush—

she was stunned to see her parents together. "What's going on?"

Her father arched a brow. "I think I should be the one asking that, don't you?"

Folding her arms across her chest, she grinned. "Nope. I'm a big girl, Daddy. Besides, I asked you first."

Leon looked to Margaret, who gave him a soft smile and a nod. He took his wife's hand.

Beth felt the instant sting of tears. She couldn't remember the last time she'd seen her parents touch. "Does this mean you talked things out?"

Leon laughed at Margaret's blush. "You could say that," he told Beth. "Your mother and I...we've decided to start over."

"You mean..." Beth's pulse thundered. "You mean you're going to stay married?"

"Stay married, and live together as man and wife. That's exactly what we mean." He and Margaret shared a long, tender look that brought Beth's tears to the surface. "Now." Leon turned back to Luke and Beth. "Suppose you tell us what the devil's going on with the two of you?"

"If you don't mind," Luke said, looking chagrined, "we'll wait a minute, so we only have to say it once." He nodded toward the front window.

At the curb Luke's entire family, including Ryan, was spilling out of all four doors of J.D.'s Lincoln.

Fighting a grin, Beth moved closer to Luke and slipped an arm around his waist.

The look he gave her was one of wry amusement. "I knew I shouldn't have answered the door."

"Well, you thought it was J.D. You were only a couple of minutes off."

In a low voice he hoped only she could hear, he said, "Do you want to get dressed before they come in?"

"Are you kidding? And deprive our grandchildren of a terrific story? They'd never forgive us."

Luke was laughing when he opened the door and invited the whole damn family inside.

When they'd all filed in—Ryan, Zach, Kat, J.D., Mike and Sandy—J.D. took one look at Luke and Beth, Beth's bare legs, Luke's blush, and started laughing.

"Ah, hell," Luke muttered.

"Golly," Ryan said, his eyes wide. "Mom? Dad? What's going on?"

Mike nudged him in the ribs. "Don't be stupid. You wanted them to get back together, didn't you?"

J.D. held his sides and laughed harder. "God, and you thought my catching you parking up at Well 12 last week was bad. This time the whole family's caught you."

Leon's gaze sharpened and zeroed in on Luke. "What's this about Well 12?"

"Never mind, Daddy," Beth said in a rush.

When J.D.'s laughter finally ended—rather abruptly as a result of a pinch on the arm from Kat—Luke looked at Beth expectantly. She gave him a smile and a slight nod.

Luke felt his insides start to quake. Like the sweaty-palmed teenager he'd once been, he turned and faced Leon, all thought of laughing gone. Wishing he had on a shirt, maybe even shoes and socks for the occasion, he rubbed his hands down the thighs of his jeans and took a deep breath. "Now that everyone's here, I guess I can say what needs saying."

"You do that." Leon's voice was gruff.

Luke met his gaze squarely. "I had this speech all memorized sixteen years ago, Leon. I was just waiting for Beth to come home before I gave it to you. Well, she's home now, and so is her mother." A wry smile curved his mouth. "But now I have to say it to Ryan, too, I think."

Beth slipped her hand in his and squeezed. The look she gave him calmed him, gave him a heady rush of welcome confidence and filled him with love. "I love your daughter, Leon—and your mother, Ryan—very much. I've loved her since I was six years old, and I've never loved anyone else, never will. I'm asking permission, from both of you, to marry her." He let his gaze settle on his son. "I want us to be a family, Ryan. A real one. I love you both more than anything in the world, and I don't want us to spend another day apart from each other."

"Well, it's about damned time," Leon whispered.

Glassy eyed, Ryan swallowed hard. His smile was big and bright and wobbly. "Oh...yeah. Oh, yeah."

*   *   *   *   *

In April 1997
Bestselling Author

DALLAS SCHULZE

takes her Family Circle series to new heights with

TESSA'S CHILD

In April 1997 Dallas Schulze brings readers a
brand-new, longer, out-of-series title featuring the
characters from her popular Family Circle miniseries.

When rancher Keefe Walker found Tessa Wyndham he
knew that she needed a man's protection—she was
pregnant, alone and on the run from a heartless past.
Keefe was also hiding from a dark past...but in one
overwhelming moment he and Tessa forged a family
bond that could never be broken.

Available in April wherever books are sold.

Silhouette SPECIAL EDITION™

That SPECIAL Woman!

**IT TAKES A VERY SPECIAL MAN TO WIN THAT
SPECIAL WOMAN... Don't miss THAT SPECIAL WOMAN!**
every other month from some of your favorite authors!

**May 1997   HUSBAND BY THE HOUR
                    by Susan Mallery (SE#1099)**

To satisfy her family, Hannah Pace needed Nick Archer to
pretend to be her husband. But this upstanding lady cop
never imagined their charade would become all too real—or
that the disarmingly sexy Nick was not who he seemed!

**July 1997   THE 200% WIFE
                    by Jennifer Greene (SE#1111)**

Abby Stanford gave her all to everything she tried. So when
she met sexy Gar Cameron, she set out to prove she'd be
the *perfect* wife. But Gar didn't want perfection...he wanted
her love—200%!

**September 1997   THE SECRET WIFE
                    by Susan Mallery (SE#1123)**

Five years ago, Elissa's dreams were coming true when she
married Cole Stephenson—but their honeymoon was short-
lived. Yet, when Elissa returned to bring proper closure to her
and Cole's relationship, she realized she *really* wanted a
second chance. Could they rekindle their love?

ERICA SPINDLER

the bestselling author of
FORTUNE and FORBIDDEN FRUIT

Outrageous and unconventional, Veronique Delacroix
is an illegitimate child of one of the oldest and
wealthiest families in New Orleans. A gambler by
nature, Veronique can never say no to a challenge...
especially from Brandon Rhodes, heir to one of the
biggest business empires in the country. Thus begins a
daring game of romantic roulette, where the stakes
may be too high....

**"Erica Spindler is a force to be reckoned with
in the romance genre."** —*Affaire de Coeur*

CHANCES ARE

Available in May 1997 at your favorite retail outlet.

At last the wait is over...
In March
New York Times bestselling author

NORA ROBERTS

will bring us the latest from the Stanislaskis as
Natasha's now very grown-up stepdaughter,
Freddie, and Rachel's very sexy brother-in-law
Nick discover that love is worth waiting for in

WAITING FOR NICK

Silhouette Special Edition #1088

and in April
visit Natasha and Rachel again—or meet them
for the first time—in

The Stanislaski Sisters

containing TAMING NATASHA
and FALLING FOR RACHEL

Available wherever Silhouette books are sold.

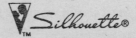